The Glass
Phoenix

The Glass Phoenix

Mary Stetson Clarke

The Viking Press   New York

For Janet

Verses on pages 148 and 149 reprinted with permission of The Macmillan Company from *South Shore Town* by Elizabeth Coatsworth. Copyright 1948 by Elizabeth Coatsworth.

Fic   1. American history
        2. Massachusetts
        3. Glassmaking

Contents

6

Foreword

To my aunt, Janet Russell Phillips, go my chief thanks for assistance in writing this book. She and her husband and small daughter lived briefly in Sandwich, Massachusetts, when I was in my early teens, and with my parents and three brothers I visited her there. From the old house on Water Street we wandered through the town, rowed on Shawme Lake and fed its ducks, picnicked and swam at the beach, and roamed around the site of the old glassworks. Still a Cape Cod resident, Janet Phillips has recently again been my guide to Sandwich, and together we have driven over early roads, visited historic houses and churches, and pored over old volumes. Her enthusiastic sharing of this interest has given a special impetus to my work.

For the help of many people in Sandwich I am grateful, especially for that of Mrs. Doris Kershaw, Curator of the Sandwich Historical Society's Glass Museum, and for her courtesy in answering many questions about the town and its famed glass factory. Miss Priscilla Harding, Librarian of the Sandwich Public Library, was also cordial and helpful, and furnished me with many out-of-print volumes about old Cape Cod. Several individuals at the office of the Board of Selectmen were kind in showing me old maps and tax books. And at the Daniel Webster Inn I found the traditional hospitality that marked the hostelry when it was Fessenden's, and was shown through the old rooms, including that occupied by the great statesman on his frequent visits.

The verses on Phoebe's sampler are taken from a piece of needlework embroidered by Margaret Ann Parker, aged eleven in 1829. It is now in the possession of her fourth namesake and great-great-granddaughter, Margaret Ann Pustell, who kindly allowed me to copy it.

I am also indebted to Elizabeth Coatsworth, in whose book of essays, *South Shore Town* (Macmillan, New York, 1948), I read of a purification party held long ago in Hingham, Massachusetts. With her permission I have adapted the ceremony and song for use in this story.

Harley P. Holden, Assistant in the Harvard University Archives, gave me information on Harvard College as it was in 1827. Richard Chesley, president of Thomas Long Company of Boston, determined the weight of an 1807 wedding ring for me.

Finally, I wish to pay tribute to the continuing interest, cooperation, and support of my friends at the Melrose Public Library.

The Glass Phoenix

Trespassers

The tall clock in the corner of the sitting room struck two sonorous bongs. Ben Tate, his lanky six-foot frame stretched across the braided rug, looked up from the fine print of the *Columbian Centinel,* and examined the clock's elaborate face. For the hundredth time he marveled that it showed, not only seconds, minutes, and hours, but the date as well—July 16. Only the year was missing—1827.

On the other side of the room Grandfather let the tilted legs of his Windsor chair thump down onto the wide floor boards. He rubbed one gnarled hand across his eyes and said, "Time to get back to the corn." Beneath his thatch of white hair his leathery face showed deep lines.

Reluctantly Ben pulled himself to his feet and laid the paper on Grandfather's desk. He wanted to finish reading about the steamboat *Patent* and the damage it had suffered in a storm between Portland and Boston. But Ezra Tate expected instant obedience from his sixteen-year-old grandson and was already moving toward the door.

The older man in the lead, they walked through the kitchen, where Ben's mother and sister were clearing up after dinner. Phoebe was four years younger than Ben and wore her blond braids tied back in a bow. She was sloshing the last of the plates in soapy dishwater. Ma was pushing a cork into the mouth of an earthenware jug with her usual deftness. Ben couldn't imagine anyone more neat and tidy than Ma, from her smooth brown hair to the hem of her crisp gingham skirt.

"Here's some switchel for you," she said. "The sun will be hot on top of the hill today."

Ben felt thirsty already at the prospect of the cool mixture of molasses and water seasoned with vinegar and ginger. Switchel was some compensation for the monotony ahead. Did Ma suspect how much he hated hoeing corn?

As he stepped off the back porch Ben could feel the sun's heat through his thick brown hair and on his muscled arms, already bronzed. Ahead of him Grandfather moved stiffly to grasp the hoe he had leaned against the wall before dinner, and set off across the pasture toward the upper cornfield.

Ben, carrying the jug and his own hoe, matched his pace to Grandfather's. The grass was springy underfoot, the air scented with the honeysuckle and roses growing along the stone walls that ridged the hillside. As they climbed, Ben looked out across the marsh to the sparkling expanse of Massachusetts Bay, hoping for a glimpse of his father's schooner. The *Orion* was due home any day now.

There was no sign of the familiar sails. Looking inland, he could see that the town of Sandwich lay in midday quiet, leafy trees arching above white houses.

Grandfather suddenly sucked in his breath. "Look there, coming from behind the barn!"

Two men, one tall and lean, the other short and squat, were cutting across the field below. The tall one carried a gun, its barrel over his shoulder as if he were on parade. The other had a bottle in his hand. He stopped, tilted back his head, and took a drink.

Ezra Tate started down the hill at a run. Even though he was seventy-six he could move speedily when he wished. Brandishing his hoe, he advanced upon the intruders.

"Where do you think you're going?" he demanded. "This is private property!" His white beard jutted out fiercely.

The man with the gun observed mildly, "Sure, and we're not harmin' your grass by just walkin' on it. Me and O'Connor are just takin' a short cut to get into the woods. Then we'll be on glassworks land." His narrow, sallow face took on an ingratiating expression, the lips curving to expose broken teeth.

"Glassworks land!" exploded Ezra Tate. "It's *my* land, every foot of it, from that fence over there on the other side of the house down to the marsh, and over the ridge. Where did you get the idea it belonged to the glassworks?" He was breathing heavily.

The short man gazed at him blandly, his eyes round in a face fringed by reddish hair. "Faith, and we'd heard that Mr. Jarves had bought up every foot of woodland in Sandwich."

Ezra Tate snorted. "Everybody else in town may have sold out to Deming Jarves, but not me. I wouldn't sell one of my trees for firewood to feed the furnaces in his danged factory." He shook a fist at the sprawling buildings on the far side of the marsh, where a plume of smoke billowed from the huge chimney. "Now, get off my property before I drive you off. I'll not have you hunting in my woods."

"Who's to say we're out hunting?" asked the stocky man. "A little target practice is all we're after."

"Have it somewhere else," said Ezra Tate with cold finality.

Ben hung back, embarrassed by Grandfather's brusque words. No wonder the newcomers were resentful when the old residents treated them in so hostile a manner.

The men turned and walked down the hill, arrogance in each unhurried step. Ezra Tate waited until they had reached the road and started for the town before he headed back toward the cornfield. Ben lingered a moment, thinking he saw someone moving behind the barn. Probably it was just a shadow thrown by the old elm tree. He turned and hurried after Grandfather, who was stamping angrily along.

"Target practice, my eye!" the older man sneered. "Those men are after deer. Danged fools haven't sense enough to wait till fall. Folks should have known the glassworks would bring trouble."

Ben said nothing. Once Grandfather got started on

Deming Jarves and the Boston and Sandwich Glass Company, there was no stopping him. Any word of assent or dissent merely prolonged the tirade.

"All these ignorant foreigners Jarves has brought in don't know how to live with decent people," Ezra went on. "Can't even write their names, some of them. Spend their pay on liquor, brawl in the streets, and beat their wives. Sandwich was a quiet, God-fearing town until they came."

It has been quiet enough, Ben thought, nearer dead. Sandwich men farmed or went to sea, except for a few who kept store or worked in the tavern. The only excitement was in the fall, when gentlemen from Boston came down for the hunting with their guns and dogs. Or in the spring, when they came for the fishing and hired Johnny Trout the Mashpee Indian to lead them to the best streams.

"The town has changed so that Daniel Webster says he's not coming any more—now that the glassworks men have ruined the hunting and fishing." Grandfather scowled at Ben. "Tell me one good thing Deming Jarves has done for this town."

Ben couldn't resist the temptation. "The Fourth of July fireworks!" he said triumphantly. He could close his eyes and still see the magnificent display of rockets and whirring fiery set pieces. On the third of July every boy who worked at the factory received a fifty-cent piece from Mr. Jarves, to be spent on fireworks and nothing else. From early dawn until midnight the town resounded with the popping of firecrackers, commemorat-

ing Independence Day and the opening of the glassworks two years before.

"A danged waste of money," spat Grandfather, "and
dangerous. It's a wonder Jarves hasn't set the town on
fire with his foolishness."

Foolishness or not, the gay display was a high point
of the year for Ben. He was almost sorry he was not a
glassworks boy with fifty cents to spend on firecrackers
and pin wheels. Most of the boys started at the factory
when they were eight, and by the time they were Ben's
age they acted so cocky and know-it-all you'd think they
ran the glassworks singlehanded. Except Martin O'Connor, who was in Ben's class at school. Ben did not know
Martin well because he kept to himself and rarely spoke
in the classroom. He worked two five-hour shifts, one beginning at seven in the morning, the other at seven in
the evening, and had only a few hours in between to attend school. It was a good thing he had every Friday and
Saturday off to catch up with the other pupils.

Those two days off at the end of the week were a sore
point with the other factory men, most of whom put in
six full days. But they all knew that anyone who worked
directly with the glass—the men who fired the giant furnace, those who fed raw materials into the huge pots,
and the glass blowers and their apprentices—had no
choice of hours. They toiled in alternating shifts around
the clock so long as the glass was workable, and they
needed the other days to rest.

When Ben and Grandfather reached the cornfield,
Ben set the jug of switchel in the shade of an old oak on
the edge of the wood lot that bordered the field, and

went to work chopping at the weeds that surrounded the young stalks of corn.

Swish! Click! The metal blade cut through chickweed and sorrel in quick rhythm. Ben worked until his throat was dry, stopped to offer Grandfather a swig of the cool drink and to take one himself, then continued his onslaught on the weeds. From the other side of the field sounded Grandfather's slow, deliberate strokes, half a dozen rows behind Ben. He'd have to think of some excuse for helping the old man finish his half of the corn before the afternoon was over.

Above the chip-chop of the hoes Ben could hear the drone of locusts, the whistles of a pair of bobwhites, and the jangle of a cowbell from the wood lot. Narcissa must have wandered off again. The cow was as foolish as the name Phoebe had chosen. Phoebe had seen the baby calf staring at its reflection in the drinking trough, and had insisted on naming it after the youth of mythology, but with the proper feminine ending to show off her scant Latin.

A sudden shot shattered the peaceful afternoon. The crash reverberated, followed by a bellow of pain and anguished bovine groans. Narcissa must have been hit!

"Those consarned idiots from the glassworks!" roared Grandfather, his face screwed up in fury. He dropped his hoe and set off stiffly toward the wood lot.

Ben followed, racing in long leaps through blueberry bushes and thorny vines, across slippery pine needles and oak leaves, toward the stentorian bellows. Up over a rise he rushed, and saw Narcissa just below, half hidden in a thicket, her legs thrashing wildly. Beside her stood the two men from the glassworks.

" 'Tis a foine deer ye've bagged for us, Tully," said the man with the round face. "What say we have a drink on it?" He reached for the bottle.

"I ask ye, O'Connor, what business has a cow got roamin' the woods like a wild beast?" asked the other, his sharp face sullen.

Ben was launching himself down the slope in fury when he heard Grandfather's hoarse cry.

"You blasted fools! If you hanker to kill something, why don't you go after wolves and get the bounty?"

Hearing the shout, the two men took off like rabbits. Ben started to follow them, but they had a good lead and in a few minutes were out of sight. When Ben returned he stared in horror at Narcissa's foreleg. Just below the knee was a bloody wound, and the leg was bent back at an unnatural angle.

"Go to the house, Ben, and fetch me my musket," ordered Grandfather, his nostrils flaring. "I'll put the poor beast out of her torment."

Ben loped down the cart track toward the house, hot with anger. He'd get the musket as ordered, but he wouldn't take it straightaway to Grandfather. First he'd find those dunderheads who'd shot Narcissa and let them see how it felt to get a ball in the leg.

Ben burst into the kitchen panting. His mother was stirring a kettle of cherry preserves at the big black stove while Phoebe set out a row of crockery jars. They looked up in alarm.

"What's happened? Is Grandfather hurt?"

"No, but Narcissa is. Some drunks from the glassworks shot her in the leg. I've come to fetch the gun to—"

Phoebe darted to Ben, her blue eyes flashing. "No! You musn't shoot her!"

Ben strode across the kitchen toward Grandfather's room. If he didn't hurry, he'd never find the men. "Don't be silly, Phoebe. You don't understand these things."

Phoebe clenched her fists. "It wasn't you fell out of the pear tree last summer and broke a leg. But nobody shot me. Whey can't Dr. Dow put a splint on Narcissa's leg?"

"Because he's not a vetcrinarian," Ben said. "Only Doc Blossom treats animals."

"Ruthie Blossom told me her Pa went to Boston on the packet yesterday," said Phoebe. "Dr. Dow's the only one in town who can take care of Narcissa. I'll run and get him. My leg's as good as ever."

Ma shoved the bubbling kettle to the back of the stove. "It seems a pity to lose such a good milker because of a broken leg."

"What would you do, put her to bed in there?" Ben pointed to the bedroom just off the kitchen where Phoebe had recuperated.

"There must be some way to keep Narcissa off that leg," said Ma.

Ben sighed. When Ma got an idea, there was no point in opposing her. He might as well give up any hope of catching the men. They were probably back in the tavern by now, boasting about what fine shots they were.

"Think, Ben. If you were on a desert island with Narcissa, what would you do?"

Into Ben's mind flashed a picture of an island, lush and green, with sea, sand, and palm trees. Slung between two tree trunks was a hammock in which he lolled at ease. And in another hammock lay Narcissa, one leg sticking out, stiff with splint and bandage. Any other time he would have laughed. But not now.

There was an old hammock under the apple tree. Could he rig it up somehow? He'd heard of canvas slings devised by sea captains on stormy voyages to prevent horses from falling and breaking their legs. And when he shod oxen the blacksmith put them in slings. If the hammock were slung crosswise under Narcissa, with holes cut in it for her forelegs, and hung from a beam in the barn, she would have a chance to recover. He described his plan.

"First we'll have to get Narcissa back to the barn," said Ma.

"Too bad it isn't winter," sighed Phoebe. "Then we could slide her over the ice."

"We could slide her on the stone boat," said Ben. Some of the boulders transported on the flat runnerless sledge weighed as much as a cow, he was sure.

A few minutes later Phoebe was running down the road to the doctor's house. Ben and his mother set off for the wood lot with the two farm horses drawing the stone boat. In her arms Margaret Tate carried a bundle of old blankets.

At the sight of the horses, Ezra Tate asked, "What

fool idea have you got now, Ben? I sent you for my gun."

Ben explained.

"It'll never work," said the old man dourly.

"Maybe not," said Ben, "but I'd like to try."

"We've got to keep her from kicking or we won't be able to budge her an inch," said Grandfather. Ben could have cheered.

Try though they might, Ben and Ezra could not hold the kicking animal still. Every time they caught the flailing legs Narcissa struck out anew with her sharp hoofs.

"If we had just one more person to help hold her," Ma said.

Behind them sounded a low cough and Ben turned to see a slight youth with a freckled face and short-cropped reddish hair step out from behind a tree. Looking at Ma, he said, "Maybe I could be of help to you, ma'am?"

What was Martin O'Connor doing here, so far from the factory village? Ben had no time to ask, for Ma said quickly, "You certainly can help. Stand over there by Mr. Tate. When he says the word, you grab for a leg and hold on for all you're worth." She looked up at the newcomer. "Just tell me your name in case I have to give a quick order."

"Martin O'Connor," said both boys at once. Ben laughed and Martin glared at him.

"I came to help, not to be laughed at," he said resentfully.

"Are you ready now?" Grandfather asked. "One, two, three—grab!"

The three reached forward and caught the hoofs.

Gently Ma took the torn limb in her hands and straightened it, talking in a soft voice.

"Now Narcissa, don't be afraid. I've watched Justin Dow enough times to know how he does this. We'll just put these two sticks here, and bind them nice and firm."

Except for one loud bellow, Narcissa was quiet. Once the splints were in place, Grandfather tied the three good legs together. Then he and Ma and the boys hauled Narcissa onto the stone boat while the horses stamped and whickered nervously.

When Narcissa was safely tied down, Martin said, "If you've no further need of me, I'll be going now."

Ma gave him a warm smile. "Won't you come home and have supper with us?"

"Thank you, ma'am, but I couldn't." Martin turned and went swiftly off through the woods.

Grandfather clucked to the horses, driving them at a slow pace, while Ben and Ma followed.

"It was a good thing that boy happened along," said Ma.

Ben was silent. He was sure that Martin's presence was no chance happening. He must have been following the glassworks men. The one named O'Connor might be Martin's father. Ben had seen them coming out of the company store one day, the man walking ahead, and Martin bent nearly double under a sack of potatoes.

The horses emerged from the woods, crossed the pasture, and soon drew up before the barn. The doctor arrived a few minutes later, with Phoebe sitting beside him in his chaise.

Dr. Dow stepped to the ground and said angrily, "Another victim of some idiots with firearms! Any chance of their being brought to justice?"

"They ran off before we could catch up with them," Ezra said furiously.

Ben opened his mouth to speak, then shut it. He had no proof that Martin had been with the hunters. He was not even sure of their identity.

"What can you expect of such irresponsible scum?" asked the doctor. He stepped over to look at Narcissa. "Weren't you a bit hasty to send for me, Margaret?" he asked Ma. "I've never treated a cow in my life."

Phoebe let out a wail. "What's the difference between an animal doctor and a people doctor?"

"A good deal," said Dr. Dow. "For one thing, I don't ordinarily have to worry about a patient kicking me." He stroked his silky dark mustache.

Ma gave the doctor a level look. "Surely you can forget your professional dignity for once, Justin. How can you just stand there when poor Narcissa needs your help?"

Dr. Dow smiled. "Don't be cross with me, Margaret. I'll be glad to look at your cow, but you appear to have the situation pretty well in hand. You've had more experience with ailing animals than I've had—or ever will, if I can help it."

He took off his coat and rolled up his shirt sleeves, then unwound the bandage and felt the injured leg. "Might as well get some water and clean it out. I'll put on some ointment and new splints."

"Will Narcissa get better?" asked Phoebe.

"If the wound doesn't fester, and if you can keep her

off that leg so the bones can knit properly," said the doctor. Ben went to the orchard and unfastened the ropes that held the hammock.

An hour later Narcissa's leg was newly splinted. Ben had cut the hammock to fit her, and she was supported by it, her hoofs clearing the barn floor by a few inches. Instead of resting quietly, however, Narcissa twisted and thrust out her legs, trying to reach the familiar floor boards. She wanted to stand on her own feet; there was no doubt about it. Nervously she proclaimed her uneasiness, bawling hard and long.

At the supper table all the family were tired and jumpy. Ma's dress soaked in a bucket of water under the sink. Despite her care the jam had burned.

Grandfather looked up from his plate in annoyance. "Don't know as I can stand any more of that caterwauling," he observed.

Ben's mind was in a turmoil. He'd have to find some way to calm Narcissa. "Maybe if I went down and talked with Ira, he'd have some idea," he said. "Would it be all right if I went over to his place tonight?"

The Incredible
Machine

The minute supper was over, Ben went out to the barn, gave Narcissa a pat, and took a final look at her sling. Then he set out for Ira's.

A quarter mile down the road, Ira Benson lived alone in his family homestead beside the marsh. He cooked and slept in the house, but most of his hours he spent in the adjoining shop. A wiry man with curly grizzled hair and beard, he walked with a slight limp caused by a childhood injury. The Bensons had come to Sandwich with other Quakers soon after the town was settled. The first Benson had a skill in woodworking that Ira had inherited, and to which he had brought great ingenuity. He was the most accomplished cabinetmaker this side of Plymouth. And he was always fussing over some device, such as a means of opening stove drafts on a cold morning without having to get out of bed. Perhaps he'd have an idea on how to keep Narcissa steady.

Ben liked this stretch of road between farm land and marsh. A southwest breeze wafted the fragrance of honeysuckle and pine. Gulls soared overhead, and a song sparrow lilted its sweet notes. The sinking sun gilded the windows of the distant meetinghouse.

Across the quiet evening rang the clear notes of a bell, the signal for the men on the evening shift to come to the glass factory. On the far side of the marsh Ben could see a straggle of figures making their way toward the glassworks. Was one of them Martin O'Connor? What a way to live, ordered about by bells—almost as bad as going to school.

As he drew near Ira's shop Ben noticed a pair of matched bays and a carriage standing outside. Only one person in Sandwich drove so stylish a vehicle, shiny with olive-green paint and yellow trim. Mr. Jarves must have ordered a piece of fine furniture from Ira.

Ben lingered on the clamshell path. He could see the two men bending over a bench—Ira in his faded work clothes, Deming Jarves, tall and fair-haired, elegant in a buff suit, holding his beaver hat in one hand. Until this minute Ben had seen Mr. Jarves only at a distance. He watched and listened. Ira was pointing to a wooden framework surmounted by a wheel and screw. As he spoke he moved his hands up, then down.

Suddenly Mr. Jarves stepped back and exclaimed, "A machine to press hollow tumblers of glass? It could revolutionize the entire glass industry. It's incredible, I say, absolutely incredible." He bent over the machine again, turning the wheel round and round. "You'll have to think of some way to depress the lever more swiftly. You can't waste a second when you're working with molten glass or it will harden."

"I'm not sure just how I could do it," Ira said hesitantly.

"You'll think of something," Mr. Jarves said in a confident tone. "As soon as you make the necessary changes, bring the machine to the carpenter shop at the factory. It will be safe there until we try it out."

Ben stepped inside the doorway, burning with curiosity. What could Ira have built that was so incredible? And why must it be taken to the carpenter shop for safety? Mr. Jarves started toward the door of the shop. Ben couldn't help noticing his eyes, bright blue, and so intense in their gaze as to command immediate attention. Ben drew back to let him pass.

Mr. Jarves paused and said, "You look like a strong young man. I don't believe I've seen you at the glassworks. Would you like a good steady job with a chance for advancement?"

"I haven't finished school yet," said Ben. He couldn't tell Mr. Jarves that his family would disown him if he so much as thought of going to work at the factory.

"When you're through with your schooling, come and see me. I'm on the lookout for likely young men to learn glassmaking." Mr. Jarves spoke the word *glassmaking* with pride, as if he thought it was the most wonderful business in the world. Then he walked briskly to his carriage, stepped in, and drove off.

Ben stood looking after him. Mr. Jarves was certainly pleasant enough—not the regal, awesome ogre Ben had expected.

Ira limped toward the doorway. "Ah, Ben, it's good to

see thee. Has something special brought thee here so late in the day?"

What was a cow compared with a machine that Deming Jarves predicted would change the entire glass industry?

"First show me what you've been working on," said Ben, walking across sawdust and shavings to the bench. He examined the machine carefully. The wheel and screw were similar to those on the paper press in Lawyer Doane's office. But instead of the metal plate which held papers in place, there was a solid cylinder directly above a larger hollow cylinder.

"Try turning the screw, Ben," said Ira. While Ben twisted the wheel Ira continued, pointing to the empty cylinder. "The glass goes in here, then the plunger comes down on top of it and forces the molten glass up and around the sides of the mold."

Ben watched the plunger descend and come to a stop. When he reversed the turn of the wheel, the plunger rose. If Ira said this device would press glass, he must be right. Still, it was hard to believe that it would work. Glass wasn't something a carpenter meddled with. Glass was something special that only glass blowers could handle. Every boy in Sandwich knew that—every boy who had dared to go near enough the doorway of the glasshouse to look in at the mysteries performed there. And after watching the swift twirling and swinging, rolling and cutting, as the glowing hot glass was passed back and forth from hand to hand, he knew beyond a doubt that glassmaking was the most highly skilled work in the world.

Ira put one hand on the press. "Mr. Jarves is right. This does work too slowly," he said. "It will require some thought." He paused, chewing on the ends of his mustache, then looked up at Ben. "Now, what has thee on thy mind?"

Ben perched on a sawhorse. "You'll never believe what happened to our cow," he said, and launched into the tale. When it was told, he added, "I thought you might help me figure out some way to make Narcissa more comfortable."

Ira clucked sympathetically. "Levers and joists I might help thee with, but the comfort of a cow—" He threw up his hands.

"If you could hear the poor thing you'd know she needs help."

"Let's think this out," Ira said solemnly. "Narcissa is unhappy because she is in the air. And she can't stand on the floor because the broken leg won't bear her weight. Could she stand on three legs?"

"Probably," said Ben impatiently, "but what about that fourth leg?"

"Thee could cut a hole in the floor under it."

"Grandfather would have a fit if I did that," said Ben. Then he asked, "Wouldn't a raised platform under three good legs do just as well?"

"That's thy answer," said Ira. "The cow's leg can swing free while it heals, and when it is better, thee can remove the platform, and there will be the level floor for her to stand on, as good as ever. Has thee enough boards?"

Ben laughed. "You know Grandfather's shed. It's

chock full of things he says might come in handy some day. He has enough boards to make twenty platforms. I'd better get home and start in on it."

He strode home through the twilight, whistling. Tonight he'd lay some boards under Narcissa so her good legs would have some support and she wouldn't swing around in the sling. Tomorrow he'd build a proper platform for her. And then he'd give some thought to Ira's machine. There must be some way to depress that plunger in a hurry.

Halfway home he realized that he'd forgotten to ask why the machine should be taken to the carpenter shop for safety.

The Pump

The next morning Narcissa was still unhappy. Her head drooped listlessly, she moaned at intervals, and she gave only half as much milk as usual. Her injured leg had swollen alarmingly. She kept moving her hoofs around on the boards Ben had shoved under her the night before. Some of them had shifted, leaving wide cracks between.

All morning Ben measured and sawed and pounded. By noontime he had put together a strong solid platform and had nailed it with spikes to the barn floor. To his relief, Narcissa now stood quietly, as if reassured by the stability of the raised wooden floor under her three sound legs.

After dinner Ma asked Ben, "What do you plan to do this afternoon?"

Ben's eyebrows rose. "What I do every day," he said. "Work with Grandfather."

"I was wondering if you could go over to Honor's and look at her pump. It's not drawing right. I worked that handle yesterday until my arm was tired, and could get only a trickle of water. With little Noah she has a lot of wash, too."

Suddenly Ben felt less tired. "I could go over this afternoon if Grandfather doesn't mind."

"The weeds'll wait. They'll be grown more, but I guess a half day won't matter," said Ezra Tate.

Ben collected some things from his workbench and set out for his older sister's home. Only a few houses stood between the Tates' weathered homestead and the white cottage to which Caleb Wilcox had brought his bride two years ago. Trim and tidy, with flower beds rimmed by quahog shells, it was just such a place as one would expect neat, careful Caleb to choose.

Honor met him on the vine-covered back porch. She must have washed her hair, he thought, for it hung loose and damp. She didn't look like a married woman of nineteen, or the mother of a year-old toddler.

"Ben, dear. How is my little brother?" This was a joke between them, since she had to stand on tiptoe to kiss his cheek.

He gave her shoulder an awkward pat. "Hot," he said, and asked, "Where's Noah? Asleep?"

"Yes, thank goodness. I thought he'd never quiet down." Some of Ben's disappointment must have shown, for she added, "He'll probably wake up before you go."

Automatically Ben glanced at the wood piled on the porch. The stack was waist-high, enough to last several days in this weather.

"I suppose you heard about Narcissa," he said.

"Yes. Phoebe came down first thing this morning. I wish somebody would do something about those terrible glassworks men." She led the way into the house. "Would you like a piece of rhubarb pie?"

"Would I?" He followed her into the cool kitchen with its crisp curtains and red-checked cloth on the center table.

"It's so warm I let the fire go out. I like a cold lunch, and can get along without anything hot for supper. It isn't as if I had a hungry man coming home." Her voice shook.

"Don't you worry, Honor. Caleb and Pa'll be along soon. They probably had to wait for a return cargo. Or they may have run into head winds."

"I know." She sat down at the table, picked up a knife, and cut into the pie.

Ben's mouth was watering. There was simply nothing to compare with the tart-sweet taste of rhubarb pie.

When he had finished eating he went over to the pump. Honor was lucky to have hers in the kitchen, and not in the yard, where it would freeze in the winter. Ben grasped the handle, lifted it, then pushed it slowly downward, his head cocked to one side as he listened. The slight wheeze was what he had expected.

Honor stationed herself at his elbow. "Do you know what's wrong?"

"The washer's gone kerphluey." He removed the screw that held the handle, unfastened the top rim, grasped the rod firmly, and pulled out the plunger. One edge of the cupped leather washer at the end of the plunger was folded back.

He loosened the screws that held the washer, removed

the circle of leather, and laid it on a piece of hide he had
brought with him.

"Have you got a pencil?"

Honor brought him one, freshly sharpened. He drew
around the old leather, then cut a new circle out of the
hide, taking care to make the edge as smooth as possible.
He screwed the new leather in place, thrust rod and
plunger carefully into the cylinder—it fitted perfectly—
replaced the rim, and attached the handle.

"Will it work now?" asked Honor.

"Just you watch."

Steadily he lifted up the handle. He could feel the resistance as the descending leather clung to the sides of
the pipe. He pushed down, then lifted up, hollow
squeaks accompanying each move. Down. Up. Down
again. There came deep groans as the pressure gathered,
then a trickle of water, a gurgle, and suddenly, with a
swoosh-swoosh, water gushed out into the black soapstone sink.

Honor clapped her hands. "The pump hasn't worked
as well in all the time we've lived here."

"Anything else need fixing?" asked Ben. It was odd
that getting things to work right could make him feel so
happy.

"The back-door key hasn't stuck once since you took
the lock apart," said Honor, "and the grandfather clock
strikes perfectly now."

"It's a real beauty of a clock. I may try to make one
like it some day." Ben picked up his tools and put them
in his pocket. "If there's nothing else, I'll be going
now."

"There is one thing, though I hate to ask you—"

Ben stepped back warily. If she said one word about hoeing her garden!

"I hear the *Thera* came in this forenoon. Maybe her crew has news of the *Orion*."

"I'll be glad to ask," said Ben heartily.

A few steps took him across the sandy road and down the bank to the marsh. He followed a path through the wiry grass to the creek and untied the painter of the skiff he kept there. His father had given it to him when he was eight, a proper possession for a seaman's son. Ben loved skimming over the water in his boat. If only he could be as happy at sea in the *Orion,* instead of turning inside out with seasickness every time the schooner rolled.

He drew the oars from beneath the thwarts, set them between the tholepins, and stroked the boat out into the middle of the creek. The tide was coming in; long streamers of eelgrass undulated along the sandy bottom. Crabs scuttled on the banks. A fresh breeze cooled the sun-warmed air, tingeing the fragrance of the marsh with salt.

Along the creek's farther curves, men poled two barges, heavily laden with cargo from a ship anchored at the harbor's mouth, toward the glass factory. At the town wharf was the *Thera,* her decks busy with men unloading hogsheads and crates.

With powerful strokes Ben pulled on the oars, and in a short time drew up alongside the *Thera.* One of the hands paused with a bale balanced on his shoulder and called out, "Hey, Ben, we saw your Pa in Philly."

"Did he say when he'd be coming home?" asked Ben, dipping his oars into the water to keep the skiff headed into the wind.

"He didn't say, but he had about half a cargo aboard. Could have set out a day or two after us."

"Thanks for the news," said Ben. He thrust the oars deep, pivoted the skiff, and with strong strokes aided by the tide, was soon far up the creek.

He stopped at Honor's house to tell her that Caleb would probably be home in a day or two. Little Noah had just wakened from his nap, his cheeks scarlet, his brown eyes long-lashed and merry. Ben poked a calloused finger into the baby's round stomach. He gurgled and caught Ben's hand.

"You're getting strong," Ben said. "How about a little walk?" He let the boy hold his fingers and paced behind him while Noah stepped bravely out, throwing back his round head, his rosy mouth with its four tiny teeth opened wide in laughter.

"I'm going to start making a set of little tools for Noah," said Ben. "He's got such a good grip, I bet he'd love a little hammer."

"He probably would," agreed Honor, "but I don't know that I'd like to have him pounding my good furniture."

"Oh, I'd give him some special blocks of wood to hammer on. And later, when he's bigger, some nails."

"The nails would probably go in his mouth. The blocks sound wonderful, though. He'd love those."

The grandfather clock struck four. "Time for me to

be getting along," said Ben. "I want to stop at Ira's on the way home."

"Take the rest of the pie to him," said Honor. "I don't believe he remembers to eat, half the time."

Ben followed her into the kitchen, the baby crawling rapidly behind. Honor wrapped a clean linen towel over the pie tin and handed it to Ben.

A few minutes later Ira was uncovering the pie and sniffing at it with delight. He set it down on a workbench littered with tools and shavings. "Won't thee share it with me now?" he asked.

"Couldn't think of it," lied Ben. "Had any new ideas for your machine?"

Ira sighed. "Not a one. How about thee?"

"I haven't had time," said Ben. "First I had to make that platform for Narcissa, and this afternoon I fixed Honor's pump. The washer had gone—" He fell silent as a picture of the pump came to his mind.

"The washer?" prompted Ira. "What was wrong with it?"

Ben didn't hear him. A handle like the one on the pump—that was what Ira needed. A pump handle exerted a good deal of force, and it worked fast. Wouldn't a similar lever work on Ira's pressing machine?

"Ira, I've got it," he exclaimed. In a few words he outlined his plan. "With that kind of handle you could press the glass before it had time to cool and harden."

Ira's face lit up. "I'll try it, Ben," he said. "In fact, I'll start right now. First I'll have to remove the depressing screw." He picked up a wrench and set to work. "Come over tomorrow," he invited. "I may need some help."

Night Attack

It was early evening of the next day before Ben could return to Ira's shop. Grandfather had decided that the hay in the west field should be cut. All day Ben had swung the big scythe, shearing broad swaths of rippling grass. Nothing smelled quite so good as new-mown hay, he decided, unless it was fresh wood shavings or bread baking.

When he went to the barn before supper he found Narcissa weak, listless, and without appetite, although she drank thirstily from the wooden bucket of water he offered.

Phoebe appeared and regarded the cow anxiously. "She probably wants to lie down. It must be hard for her to stand up all the time."

"We'll just have to make believe she's one of those horses on board ship," said Ben. "If they could stand it for six weeks, I guess Narcissa can."

"I hope so," said Phoebe. She laid her hand softly on the swollen leg. "I think maybe it's a little better."

Supper over and the wood box filled, Ben set out for Ira's. It was odd how light he felt when he was going to see Ira. No matter how hard he had worked during the day he forgot about being tired once he was on the way to his neighbor's workshop.

Ira was fastening a screw that held two long, narrow pieces of wood together.

"Ah, thee's come just in time," he exclaimed. "If thee would hold this in place here"—he poised the wooden pieces over the cylinders—"while I measure the distance here"—he pointed to a support—"then it should be finished."

"You've done all this today?" Ben regarded the neatly fitted levers and braces.

"I worked late last night," said Ira. "This morning I went to see Mr. Jarves and told him about the new lever, and he wants to try out the machine tomorrow. He gave me the key to the carpenter shop at the factory, and asked me to take the machine there tonight."

"Why couldn't you take it down in the morning?"

Ira's frown was troubled. "Mr. Jarves has some idea the glassworks men might try to stop me. He told me to wait till after dark. I tell thee, Ben, I don't like this secrecy. It makes me feel as if my machine was a thing to be ashamed of."

"You ought to be proud of it," said Ben. He examined the device again. "That looks pretty heavy. Would you like me to help you take it to the factory?"

"I'd be grateful if thee would. I'd thought to put it on the low wagon, but I can't move the machine on and off by myself. Now let's get this part adjusted and then fasten the handle in place."

The two worked silently for a time, so accustomed to

doing things together that they had no use for words. Ben handed tools to Ira as he needed them, knowing whether a screw driver, drill, or wrench was necessary. Ira halted once to light the whale-oil lamp that stood in a wall bracket, and the lantern that hung from a rafter. At last he straightened up and said, "Thee try it, Ben. Thee thought of the pump handle."

Solemnly Ben took hold of the wooden lever. He pressed down with a rapid motion. The plunger descended at once, almost disappearing inside the cylinder below. He lifted the handle, and the plunger emerged.

"It works, Ben! It works!" Ira cried. "Can't thee see a blob of glass in there, pressed as quick as that into a drinking glass? It will mean a wondrous saving in time and labor." His face beaming, Ira worked the lever several times. "Let's cover it up and be on our way," he said.

The wagon was a low, wheeled wooden affair that Ira had built for moving heavy objects around his workshop. He and Ben took turns drawing it along the sandy road through the quiet night. Lamp-lit windows glowed beside the tree-lined way, with curtains billowing outward in the soft summer breeze. Beside the pond the gristmill bulked gloomily. The church's white spire pointed a ghostly finger upward.

From the open door of Fessenden's tavern came the tinkle of glassware and the rise and fall of voices. Ben and Ira went on between clustered houses and dark shops through the center of Sandwich and down Dock Lane toward the glass factory.

Ahead was the company store, a solid brick building

with large windows through which light shone. A girl with black hair and a long starched apron was sweeping the porch. A few men in shirt sleeves were gathered near the steps, talking.

As Ben and Ira drew near, one of the men called out, "Will ye look at the wee wagon? And what do ye suppose they might be carrying on that, now?"

"A nice keg of rum, maybe?" suggested another, waving a pipe.

"Or a barrel of oysters. There's nothing like a good feed of oysters to satisfy a man." The speaker unhooked his thumbs from his suspenders and patted his stomach.

The first man left his companions and walked toward Ira. He was short and stout, and smelled strongly of liquor. Laying a hand on the canvas, he asked roughly, "What ya got hid under here?"

"Something Mr. Jarves asked me to deliver," said Ira.

"Fer His High Mightiness himself?" asked the man. "This could be the machine that Jerry O'Connor was talkin' about." He tugged at the cover.

"Take your hands off it," said Ben, wondering if Jerry could be the same O'Connor he had encountered two days ago.

"Will ye look at who's talkin'," said the man. "A young fightin' cock! Shall we teach him how to speak to his betters?" He waved an arm to the men on the steps, who began to move toward the wagon.

"Let's get along," said Ira in a tense voice. He limped ahead while Ben followed reluctantly. The man guffawed and returned to the group by the store.

Ben was fuming as he hauled the wagon. He hated to

look as if he were running away. But he couldn't take on the whole crowd, and Ira wouldn't lift a finger to fight. No Quaker would.

"There was a man just outside Mr. Jarves's office when I left there this morning," said Ira. "He must have overheard us talking and spread the word about my machine. He seemed downright unfriendly."

"Was he short and round-faced with reddish hair?" asked Ben.

"That's right," said Ira. "How did thee know?"

"He's the same troublemaker who came on our land with the man who shot Narcissa," explained Ben.

About a hundred feet ahead, the factory was alive with light and activity. The glasshouse door stood open to the cool evening air, and inside men and boys moved back and forth in quick bursts of activity, waving molten glass through the air like torches.

"The carpenter shop is down this way," said Ira, pointing to the left. "It's near the packing shed, handy for the crates and barrels the men knock together."

Ben turned down a lane that seemed very dark after the bright area near the glasshouse. "Just a little way farther," Ira said. "Ah, there's the doorway."

Ben let the handle of the wagon fall to the ground and waited for his eyes to get accustomed to the gloom. He could hear the scratch of metal on metal as Ira fumbled with the key, then the grating of the lock.

Suddenly, out of the blackness, a lantern appeared. A burly form approached, and a man laid a heavy hand on Ben's shoulder.

"I've caught ye red-handed," he said gruffly, swinging

the lantern up to Ben's face. "All ready to make off with some fancy tools, be ye? Or maybe it's glass ye're after?"

"Is thee the watchman?" asked Ira.

"So there be two of ye. Faith and I didn't see the other. Yes, I'm the watchman. Stand where ye are or I'll blow me whistle."

"Mr. Jarves told me to look out for thee," said Ira. "He said he'd tell thee I was going to deliver something tonight." Was Ben imagining it, or was his voice less calm than usual?

"I was lookin' out for a horse and wagon. That's how I missed ye," said the watchman cheerfully. "A nice little baby truck ye've got there." He held the lantern near the canvas wrapping, peering curiously at the strange shape. "Want I should give ye a hand lifting that in?"

"Ben and I can manage," said Ira shortly.

"I'll get on with me rounds, then. Maybe I'll look in on ye when I come back." The watchman departed, whistling.

Ira walked to the rear of the wagon, untied the ropes, and asked, "Is thee ready?"

Ben hooked his fingers under the edge of the platform that held the machine. He was about to lift when there was the thud of running feet, a muffled shout, and three men came out of the night and threw themselves onto Ben and Ira. Ben was struck a blow across the mouth, his feet caught on the wagon handle, and he fell over backward. His head hit the ground with a crack, and for a moment he lay still, his ears ringing. Groggily he tried to rise, and felt his arms pinned from behind. A few feet away a man was brandishing his fists at Ira.

"Put up yer dukes, ye spalpeen, and fight like a man!" he snarled.

Ben licked his lips and tasted blood. "Leave him alone," he cried angrily. "He can't fight. He's a Friend."

"A friend of whose, I'm askin'? Is he a friend of yours, Tully?"

"No friend of mine, O'Connor. Want I should give him a belt fer ye?" The man swung, and Ira toppled over.

Ben struggled to his feet, trying to free his arms. "Don't hit him," he roared. "He's a Quaker. It's against his religion to fight."

"Is that a fact?" asked the man called Tully. "I wonder, is it against his religion to show us what he's got here that's so important it has to be delivered at night?" He bent over the machine.

Ben kicked out with all his might at the man, and at the same time threw himself backward against his captor. The first man went sprawling, and the second lost his balance and let go his hold on Ben's arms. Ben sprinted toward the glasshouse, and as he rounded the corner, ran full tilt into the watchman.

"Three men—down there—they jumped on us," Ben panted.

The watchman put a whistle to his lips and blew a shrill blast. Then he ran forward, clutching his lantern in one hand and pulling a club from his back pocket with the other.

"Get away from Mr. Jarves's property, ye damned meddlers," he called out. There was a scuffle down the lane, the sound of running feet, and then silence.

Ben and the watchman found Ira pulling himself painfully upright.

"Are you all right?" asked Ben.

"Right enough," said Ira, "but I don't know about the machine. Look!"

Ben's heart sank. By the light of the lantern he could see that the wagon was empty. Beside it lay the machine, its canvas covering torn off. The watchman circled around it, holding the light close and saying, " 'Tis an odd thing, sure, to be fightin' about."

"How badly do you think it's damaged?" Ben asked Ira. He could see that one of the supports was broken.

"I can't tell till I can set it up in a good light. Help me get it inside."

"I'll give ye a hand," said the watchman. He set his lantern just inside the open doorway. Together the three lifted the machine and set it down in the shop. Ira drew the wagon in beside it and turned to the watchman.

"Could I borrow thy light for awhile?"

"For how long?"

"Until daylight."

"I'll be needin' it when I call the men out for the one o'clock shift, but ye can have it after that, and welcome," said the man.

"I thank thee for coming to our aid, and I'll thank thee again when thee comes back with the lantern," said Ira.

"Do you mean you're going to spend the night here?" asked Ben.

At Ira's nod of assent, he added, "Do you want me to stay?"

"Not unless thee doesn't want to go home alone. Those men may still be looking for us."

Ben hesitated. He was bruised and tired. His head ached from the fall, and his mouth pained. He had no desire to be involved in another fight. There was nothing he'd like better than to lie down on the floor of the shop and sleep. But Ma would worry if he did not come home. "I'd better go," he said softly. "I'll cut across the marsh. It's quicker, and nobody will be looking for me there."

In the darkness he felt Ira's handclasp. "If thee could bring my tools down tomorrow, I'd be thankful. I might need thy help, too. Does thee think thy grandfather would mind thy working with me here?"

Ben swallowed. Grandfather would have a fit if he suspected Ben had so much as gone near the glass factory. But Ira was his friend, and in need. "I'll try to come," said Ben.

Then he was out the door and edging along in the black shadows next to the buildings until he came to the creek. The tide was low. Good. He dropped to all fours and crept beside the water, just under the bank, until he was well away from the factory. Then he started across the marsh, bent nearly double so that he would be less visible. Not until he had waded across the small creek near his home did he stand upright. Even then he did not run. He was tireder than he'd ever been in his life.

Suspicion

Ben woke the next morning to dense fog. The air in his room was cold and damp, the curtains hung limp, and the windows were filled with a gray mist. He touched the lump on the back of his head and ran his tongue around his stiff lips. He'd surely have some explaining to do. But when he looked in the wavy mirror over his chest of drawers, he could see little change in his appearance. Same rough thatch, same big nose and teeth. Only his mouth showed a slight swelling. Maybe nobody would notice.

From below he could hear the rattle of stove lids as Ma started breakfast. He jerked on his shirt and trousers, still wet from the creek last night. When he passed through the kitchen, he kept his face averted and gave a mumbled reply to his mother's cheerful "Good morning."

Narcissa seemed a little brighter. She turned her head at his approach and gave a low moo-oo. She didn't give as much milk as before the accident, but she seemed less perturbed than yesterday. Again Ben's anger flared;

he'd like to get even with those crazy fools who had shot her. He could swear they were the same two who had jumped on him and Ira last night. Although he had not been able to see their faces clearly, he knew that one man was short and stout, the other tall and lean. And their voices and names were the same.

Softly through the fog came the muffled clang of the glass-factory bell. The carpenters would be coming to work now, and would find Ira and the machine in their shop. Had Ira slept at all? He must be exhausted and hungry. Somehow Ben must get food to him.

There were fresh raspberries for breakfast, bowls of porridge, and thick slices of homemade bread. Ben kept his head down and ate fast, but not fast enough to deceive Phoebe.

"Oooh, look at Ben's mouth. It's all puffed up."

"It's nothing," said Ben, trying to keep his lips pulled in and chew at the same time. He glared at her fiercely. Little busybody!

"It looks pretty sore," said Ma sympathetically. "How did it happen?"

"While I was helping Ira last night," said Ben shortly.

"I don't see why you spend so much time down in Ira's dusty old shop," said Phoebe. "I should think you'd want to be with some of the boys, like Billy Stetson or Jimmy Jarves."

"Those babies," sputtered Ben. "They're not more than twelve. I've got more important things to do—like splitting wood, right now." He wiped his mouth with his napkin, wincing as the linen touched his lips, and hurried out the back door.

At the woodpile he set a thick pine stick on end on the chopping block, and—*whish!*—down came his ax, splitting the pine neatly in two. Ben picked up the pieces and halved first one, then the other, with swift blows. Again and again he repeated the process until a mound of sticks encircled the block. He hung the ax in the shed out of the wet, then carried the wood, an armload at a time, to the wooden box beside the stove in the kitchen.

Grandfather was sitting at the kitchen window, a piece of harness in his hands.

"What do you have in mind for today?" Ben asked. Whatever it might be, he'd hurry through it as fast as possible so he could go and help Ira.

"It's too wet to work in the hayfield or garden," observed Ezra Tate. "A day like this is good for setting in new shingles. There's a place near the foundation on the shed where the old shingles are nigh rotted away. I had in mind setting in some new ones, but this dampness makes my joints creak. Think I'll just stay here where it's warm and dry, and mend this bridle." He looked at Ben from under bushy brows. "You want to tackle those shingles by yourself?" he asked.

Any other day Ben would have agreed. Today he was less than eager. "By tomorrow the wood will be damper and easier to work with," he said. "Would you mind if I gave Ira a hand today?"

"Seems like Ira's been needing a lot of help lately," commented Grandfather. "You could be in worse company, though. Go along."

Ben was so elated he nearly shot through the door,

The Glass Phoenix

but just in time he remembered food for Ira. "Would you mind if I took some lunch with me?" he asked his mother.

She shook the soapy water from her hands into the dishpan. "Here's the rest of this fresh loaf," she said, "and a jar of preserves. Get a stick of herrings out of the shed, and a couple of cucumbers from the garden. That ought to hold you till suppertime. Take enough for Ira, too."

After a brief stop at Ira's shop Ben hurried on. The road to the village seemed unfamiliar in the thick fog. He longed to cut across the marsh, but with all landmarks blotted out he might very easily lose his way.

Along the silent, eerie road he walked, past quiet houses and deserted fields. At the pond the rhythmic swish and drip of the gristmill's water wheel sounded strangely loud. Even Fessenden's tavern, usually a center of noise and activity, seemed subdued this morning.

As he neared the factory village he saw signs of life. The company store was open. A lamp burned inside, and a man in shirt sleeves was arranging a display of straw hats, parasols, and fans in the window, as if he were confident that sunny weather would return. The girl Ben had seen the night before brought a basket of summer squash out and set it on the steps. She was wearing a man's long apron tied tightly around her brown dress. When she saw him looking at her, she hurried into the store. He hadn't meant to stare, but she did look odd in that apron.

The one place that seemed fully awake was the glass factory. Fair weather or foul, men fed its fires, smoke poured from its chimneys, and workers bustled about their tasks. Ben paused a moment at the doorway of the glasshouse, fascinated anew by the continuous quick movement of the workers, then hurried on to the carpenter shop.

Two men were nailing slats together to form packing cases. A third was fitting legs into a bench. And a fourth was planing long boards, the shavings curling up out of the tool.

Near the doorway stood the pressing machine. Ira was bent over it, loosening the screws that held the jagged remains of the broken handle. His face lit up when he saw Ben. There was a bruise on his cheek, and one eye was swollen nearly shut.

"Did thee bring my tools?" he asked eagerly.

Ben handed him a long bundle wrapped in canvas. "I put some stock in, too. Didn't know if there'd be any hardwood on hand here."

"Good," said Ira. "I thought of that after thee had gone. I guess thee got home all right," he added guardedly.

Ben nodded in assent. "Did you sleep at all?"

"A little," said Ira. He unwrapped the tools and selected a wrench.

The four men had stopped their work and moved toward Ben. "Did Mr. Jarves send you down here, too? What's the idea? Don't he like the way we do our work?" asked one, a straw-headed giant.

"He's a friend of mine, helps me out now and then. Don't worry about your jobs. We'll be out of here as soon as Mr. Jarves is ready to try out the machine." Ira smiled in his disarming way.

A thin-faced man snickered, "You mean to say Jarves is going to waste his time on that? Ha!"

His laughter was echoed by a beefy-jowled fellow. "I know enough about glass to tell ye that this contraption can't do a gaffer's work." He slapped his knee in emphasis.

Another man, shifty-eyed, remarked, "Ye must be the feller Jerry O'Connor was talking about. Said he heard ye talkin' with the big boss about an idee. He says it's a plot to throw the glassmakers out of work."

Ben and Ira exchanged glances.

"Jerry must be right," exclaimed the light-haired man. "I was afeerd of somethin' like that when I found this chap here today. He's after yer job, I says to meself. But no, 'tis bigger game he's after, no less than the work of the glass blowers, the best paid men of all." His voice rose to a high pitch, his eyes glittered, and he swung his hammer in a menacing way.

Ira stepped in front of the machine. "Just a minute," he said in his quiet, compelling manner. "Do I look like a man who'd want to put anyone out of work? I'm a carpenter, like thyself. This is just a thing I've been tinkering with, and I wondered if it would work. The last thing in the world I want is to take a man's job away from him. Why should I? I've got my own work, and I like it, and I'd better get on with it now and finish, so I can leave here and stop cluttering up thy shop."

The man lowered his hammer. The others stood around restively.

"Say, Ben," said Ira suddenly, "what's that in thy pocket—a cucumber? And sticking out of that paper— herring? And a loaf of bread? Looks like enough to go around. How about a little snack for us all before we go back to work?"

Ben laid out the food. It was a pity to see Ira's breakfast and lunch for them both disappear so fast, but the food seemed to appease the men.

The Trial

About one o'clock the olive-green carriage drove up to the carpenter shop. As Mr. Jarves stepped to the ground he said to his coachman, "Come back in an hour, but don't call at my office. Wait for me just outside the glasshouse." A moment later he was examining the machine.

"Well, Benson, I see you got it here safely," said Mr. Jarves, "and you've brought young Tate along."

Ben could feel his chest swelling. Mr. Jarves had remembered his name.

Pulling a gold watch from his vest pocket, Mr. Jarves said, "It's time for the afternoon move. Let's get the machine into the glasshouse. You men"—he gestured to two of the carpenters—"give Benson a hand here."

While Mr. Jarves led the way the four lifted the machine and carried it down the lane and around the corner through the doorway of the glasshouse. The first thing Ben noticed was the heat. It was like a living force that met him the minute he stepped inside. His skin burned, his nostrils dried, and his lungs ached.

The heat came from a huge circular furnace in the center of the room. Into it were set eight gigantic clay pots with small openings near the top, where intense light glowed. Men poked long iron rods into these pots, dipped up portions of the red-hot viscous mass, and carried them to other men stationed at various parts of the room, twirling the rods as they walked in order to keep the molten glass from falling to the floor.

Nearby was a smaller furnace with openings on all sides from which flames danced. Here men carried partially finished articles, plunged them into the fire, then withdrew them after a brief period for further working.

Mr. Jarves led the way to an open space near a side wall. "Set the machine down here," he ordered. When it was in place, he said abruptly to the carpenters, "That will be all. You may go back to your regular work now."

Ben had never been so hot. He could feel sweat trickling down his back. He watched Mr. Jarves take off his coat, fold it neatly, and lay it on a bench. The sleeves of his fine white linen shirt clung damply to his arms.

"You're sure your machine will operate, Benson?" asked Mr. Jarves.

In reply Ira depressed the lever, then raised it.

"You've got to use more force than that. It's molten glass you'll be pressing, man." Mr. Jarves ran his eyes over Ira's slight form, and then he looked appraisingly at Ben. "I'm sure you know how the device works, Tate. I want you to man the lever. Remember, once that glass falls into the open cylinder, work fast! Molten glass congeals very rapidly. So when you press that handle down, put your back into it." He turned away, saying over his shoulder, "I'm going to take a look at the melt to see if it's ready. Wait where you are."

Ben's first thought was for Ira. Was he disappointed not to be the first to use the device? One glance at Ira's face, expectancy shining through fatigue and bruises, gave him his answer.

"A good thing thee came along, Ben," he said warmly. "I wouldn't want my machine worked by someone who doesn't understand it."

Evidently there would be some delay, for Mr. Jarves was peering into one of the openings of the furnace, and talking with a man who held a long iron rod.

The next moment Ben saw a box on wheels coming through a doorway on the far side of the room. The man pushing it was short and lumpy, and his moon face was sullen. Ben stared at him hotly. He suspected that Jerry O'Connor was one of the men who had jumped on him and Ira last night, and a purple bruise on Jerry's cheek looked like proof of it. Ben stepped back beside the pressing machine and watched O'Connor shovel the cart's contents into one of the huge clay pots.

Nearby a workman dipped a long iron pipe into a pot of molten glass, drew out a crimson blob, and blew into the pipe until the blob expanded into a bubble, which he rolled back and forth on an iron table. He handed the pipe to a man sitting in a chair with long extended arms, who with his left hand rolled the pipe back and forth on the arms. With his right hand he picked up a tool like a huge pair of tweezers and pressed it against the bubble, changing the end to a point and then a stem. To this another workman added a piece of molten glass, which was soon formed into a foot. The glass had taken on the shape of a vase.

A wiry boy touched a heated iron rod to the foot and carried the vase to the smaller furnace, thrust the vase into the fire, and stood waiting.

Ben knew Martin O'Connor worked somewhere in the factory, but he was surprised to come across him so soon. After a short time Martin drew the vase from the furnace and passed in front of Ben. He made no sign of recognition, but with one quick motion bore his red-hot burden to a man in another chair, who twirled, shaped, and smoothed the glass. The rod was then removed, and Martin carried the finished vase to an ovenlike structure.

When Ira and Ben had entered the glasshouse all the workers were going at top speed. While they waited, activity gradually slowed. As each group completed an object its members made no effort to begin another but drew near the machine. Ben looked into a circle of sullen faces.

In the sudden quiet, Mr. Jarves looked up, his amazement clear. "Why, may I ask, are you stopping your work? Time is money, you know." His tone was pleasant but commanding.

"We're wantin' to see what that contraption can do," offered a barrel-chested man, his lower jaw outthrust.

"Yea. What need have we of a thing like that?" questioned another.

"The tools we've got were good enough for our grandsirs," shouted a third.

Mr. Jarves shrugged his shoulders. "There's nothing

to get wrought up about. This is merely a device Benson
and I are working on to press glass in a hollow shape."

"Press glass that's hollow inside? Ye'll never do it!
That takes a man with a blowpipe," shouted the barrel-
chested man.

Mr. Jarves raised his hands for quiet. "Pressing glass
is not a new idea. Look at the pressed doorknobs and
salt dishes that have been on the market for years. Now
stand back, and let's see if this mechanism will operate
as we intend."

He gestured to the man with the long iron pipe. "All
right, Jenkins, you may proceed."

Ben grasped the wooden lever of the machine, every
muscle tense in readiness. Ira shot him an encouraging
smile.

Jenkins was a short man with enormously long, strong
arms. He plunged his rod into the pot of glass and
pulled forth a round, fiery blob. One step, two, and he
swung the molten glass over the open mold, then with a
swift movement shook the red-hot mass directly into the
opening. Smoke rose from the mold with the smell of
charring wood.

"Now! Press down!" roared Mr. Jarves.

With all the strength at his command, Ben swung
down on the lever, forcing the small cylinder into the
one beneath it. He could feel the resistance as the
plunger struck against the molten glass.

"Lift up! Up!" cried Mr. Jarves.

Ben raised the lever, his heart thumping. Smoke
poured from the opening.

Impatiently Mr. Jarves beckoned to Martin. "Take out the glass, O'Connor. Gently, now."

With his pronged stick Martin lifted an object from the mold and held it aloft. Its shape was thick and clumsy, its design crude, but it was plainly a hollow vessel that would hold liquid—a passable drinking glass.

For a moment there was quiet; then Deming Jarves cried out in triumph, "By Jove! It works!"

Martin moved swiftly to the oven with the tumbler and placed it inside.

Angry voices rose from the circle of men.

"It works too damned good, if you ask me," said the long-armed man.

"Good enough to do our jobs for us," shouted another.

"And throw us all out of work," added Jerry O'Connor, who had joined the group.

Ira moved close to Ben, his thin body trembling. "I don't like this, Ben. I don't like it at all," he said in a low voice.

Mr. Jarves raised his head in an imperious gesture. "It's time to get back to work. You can finish this move before the next shift comes on."

Three men started toward their places. The others remained, staring at the machine.

"Why should we work on this batch when we'll soon be thrown out of our jobs?" cried a sunken-cheeked man.

"And our wives and children will be starvin'," added another.

A man darted out of the circle, picked up a long iron bar, and raised it over his head. " 'Tis all the fault of that contraption!" he roared. " 'Tis a device of the devil!"

"Wait a moment," said Jarves, his voice cool as steel. "If you'll use your heads you'll see there's absolutely no similarity between the product of this machine and the hand-blown wares you men turn out. No one expects a machine to match the skills that it takes a glass blower years to acquire."

"Ye're damned right it takes years," burst from the barrel-chested chap. "Since I was nine years old I've been burnin' me lungs out in a glasshouse. And fer what? So a tinkerin' carpenter could yank me trade out from under me." He took a step toward Ira, brandishing a scarred fist.

Shouts arose.

"All me life I've been learnin' me trade. Damned if I'll let a machine take it away from me!"

"Takin' the bread out of the mouths of babes, it is!"

The man with the bar poised it over the machine. "Let's fix this blasted thing so it won't harm us," he bellowed.

Other voices joined his. "Smash it! Smash it!"

The workmen surged forward, a threatening mass of angry faces and upraised tools.

Deming Jarves stepped behind Ben and Ira. "I am going to leave," he said in a strained voice, "and I advise you to do the same." He stepped backward behind a pillar, then took a circuitous route through the dimly-lighted perimeter of the chamber to the doorway. Ben saw him climb into his carriage and drive away.

Ira, shocked into immobility, was standing in stunned

silence behind the machine. Should they try to save it? Ben looked frantically around for a weapon. There was none within reach. The crowd of workmen moved closer.

Crash! The man with the iron bar brought it down across the main lever. It splintered under the blow.

Whang! Another man struck with an iron rod. The plunger broke off.

Ben put his hand on Ira's shoulder. "Let's get out of here," he said through clenched teeth.

Ira stood stock still, as if in a stupor.

Ben grabbed his upper arm. "Ira, we've got to go. Come on." Half lifting the smaller man off his feet, Ben pulled him behind a pillar and into the shadows along the same route Mr. Jarves had taken. Behind them the men were going wild, smashing the machine to bits.

As they neared the door Ben heard a cry. "Get the carpenter. He's the one who started all this!"

The barrel-chested man started after them at a run. He had taken but a step or two when he tripped and stumbled. It all happened so quickly that Ben was not sure, but he thought that he saw Martin throw a rod under the man's feet.

Ben didn't wait any longer. Pulling Ira behind him, he burst out the door and into the fog. Its cool damp was a welcome relief. He took a deep breath and started to run, still holding tightly to Ira's arm.

"Thee go on, Ben. I can't keep up," Ira gasped in pain.

Ben slowed instantly. How could he have forgotten

Ira's lameness? "You can make it, Ira. Let's duck down this lane, behind these buildings. Maybe they won't see us in the fog."

Ira was limping badly, and panting. To Ben their pace seemed immeasurably slow. From behind them came shouts and the sound of running feet.

Emily

In the white mist ahead Ben could make out a slender figure in a long apron tugging at a crate. On the left was an open doorway that led into a room piled high with boxes and barrels.

"In here," said Ben. He shoved Ira ahead of him and into a corner behind a hogshead. A few minutes later a young girl backed in through the doorway, dragging a crate. She pushed the door shut and slid a bar across it, then walked softly across the storeroom and through an inside doorway, which she left open behind her. Ben could see that it led into the company store.

From the alley outside came thudding footsteps and cries.

"I saw them go down this way, along here."

"That lame fellow couldn't get very far."

"They must be somewhere near."

The sounds grew faint, then died away. Ben stood up.

"Let's get out of here," he said. There was nothing he hated more than the feeling of being trapped.

They had started toward the door when they heard the crowd returning. In a few minutes there was a thumping from outside, and a man called out, "Open up! We know you're in there."

Fear prickled up and down Ben's spine. Men who were wrought up enough to wreck a machine might do even more harm to those who had built it. He tiptoed back to the hogshead and made himself as small as possible behind it. Ira did the same behind another.

The pounding continued. A thin man with a drooping mustache walked slowly from the front part of the store to the rear door.

"Come around to the front if you've anything to say," he called out. "I have customers to attend to." With the same deliberate step he walked back through the storeroom and into the shop.

After a muffled consultation the group moved around the building. Soon a gruff voice sounded from the front of the store. "You seen anything of two men, Mr. Griswold?"

"I've seen a lot of men today. Do you mean anyone in particular?" His tone was measured.

"A little man with a limp, and a tall fellow with a mop of black hair. They're dangerous."

"Yeah. Takin' the bread out of our children's mouths, they are."

Mr. Griswold paused, as if deep in thought. "A tall man with black hair? There's one over there looking at fishhooks. Is he the one?"

"That's just Jamie O'Rourke. The guy we're after

ain't a factory man. He's from the town, a carpenter's helper. And the little chap's his boss."

Mr. Griswold's tone became brisk. "Sorry, I haven't seen anyone who answers your description. You'd better look elsewhere. And now, if you'll excuse me, I'll get back to business." There was a pause, a thump, and a squeak of scales. "There, Mrs. Flanagan, that's just one ounce over a pound. Will you have anything else besides butter today?"

"No, thank 'e," a woman said.

"I'll just take a look in the back room anyway," announced the gruff voice. Ben crouched even lower, hardly daring to breathe as the floor boards creaked under a heavy tread.

"Someone's running down the street." The clear tones sounded like a young girl's. "Could that be the person you're after?"

"Where? Which way?" The heavy boots clumped away. There was a rush of feet, then quiet.

For a long time Ben lay still. He and Ira were safe, at least for a while. Cautiously he stretched out on the worn planks.

Ira whispered, "What shall we do now, Ben?"

"Stay here till dark, I guess, then cut for home."

While they waited they listened to the comings and goings of people in the store, purchasing pickles, flour, calico, fishlines, and buttons.

Finally the girl said, "Why don't you go home and have your supper, Papa? Aunt Cassie will have it ready now."

"Don't you want to go first, Emily?"

So her name was Emily. Ben turned it over in his mind, liking its sound.

"I'm not hungry yet. I can wait till you come back."

"Very well, my dear." The front door opened and closed, and there was silence.

Suddenly a light shone in the storeroom and drew near. A youthful voice called, "You can come out now."

Ben rose cautiously to his feet. The girl stood in the main aisle, peering to left and right. She held a lamp high, and its light shone on her pale skin and fine features. Her eyes were very dark and very bright.

"I think it will be safe for you to go now," she said. "You'd better hurry, though. The next shift will be coming to work in a little while, and someone would surely see you."

Ira crept out into the light. "Thee's a brave little thing," he said. "Wasn't thee afraid we might hurt thee?"

The girl smiled. "Not of him." She looked straight at Ben. "I see him every Sunday in church."

Ben looked at her, puzzled. Last night was the first time he'd ever seen this girl, as far as he could remember.

"Oh, you can't see me," said the girl. "I sit up in the back balcony with the choir. But you're always there in the seventh pew with your mother and sisters and a man with white hair."

"You're never around after church," stammered Ben. That was when folks visited and swapped bits of news.

"I go out the back way so I can hurry home and help get Papa's dinner ready," said Emily. She gave a sudden exclamation and looked over her shoulder. "Oh, bother, there's someone coming into the store."

Ben and Ira ducked behind some crates.

Emily continued softly, "I'll shut the door after me, and you go right away, quick as you can." Picking up a basket of clothespins, she called out, "I'm just getting some stock. I'll be right there." The light faded, the door clicked shut, and the storeroom was dark. Only then did Ben realize that Emily had not asked why they were hiding.

Ben and Ira groped their way to the door, lifted up the heavy bar, and stepped cautiously out into the night. The air was still thick with fog. Silently they crept to the marsh and began their slow progress across it. Ben was too tired to worry about losing his way. With Ira at his side he plodded doggedly onward. When they came to the creek he felt a brief triumph, but when they arrived safely at Ira's house, he could feel only relief.

As they rested on the stone doorstep Ben said, "Don't feel bad about your machine, Ira. I'll help you build another."

Ira let his head fall forward onto his hands. His words, when they came, were muffled. "Thanks, Ben, but thee needn't bother. I'd thought my machine would help people by saving them toil. Now I see it might be more of a trouble than a help. Thee knows I wouldn't want to put men out of work, or cause their families to go hungry."

Ben could hardly speak for surprise. "Oh, Ira, you heard what Mr. Jarves said. The machine could never equal a glass blower's skill."

"Other men might improve my machine until it could make glass as well as the blowers. You saw what happened today. I'll have no part in causing further violence and destruction if I can help it. No, Ben, I'll not be building another pressing machine. It's a matter of conscience."

The Prisoner

The family was gathered around the dining-room table when Ben reached home. He slid into his place just as Grandfather cleared his throat, looked around warningly, and bent his head to say, "Heavenly Father, we give Thee thanks, and ask that we may be guided by Thee."

The familiar words fell on Ben's ears with a special significance. He certainly felt in need of guidance. His mind was whirling with conflicting ideas, for, like Ira, he had thought the machine a helpful device. Mr. Jarves must think so, too, or he would not have encouraged Ira to finish it and try it out. But the glassworks men were afraid of it, and in their fear they had destroyed it. He wished he could talk the whole thing over with someone experienced—his father or grandfather, perhaps. But Pa was at sea, and just mentioning the glass factory to Grandfather would be disastrous. He'd probably forbid Ben ever to set foot near the place again. Not that he wanted to—at least, not for a long time.

His mother handed him a plate filled with savory

stuffed fish, new potatoes, and fresh greens with a dollop
of butter. Food had never tasted better; he was empty to
his toes. It seemed years ago that he had eaten bread and
herring in the factory.

"Too bad you were stuck in Ira's shop all day," said
Phoebe pityingly. "You missed all the excitement."

"What happened?" asked Ben. Let her think he'd
been in Ira's shop all day if she wanted to.

"It was terrible," said Phoebe, her blue eyes wide.
"Abba Stetson and I were so frightened we ran into her
house and watched from the parlor windows."

"Was there a dog fight?" It didn't take much to get
girls squealing.

"Much worse," said Phoebe dramatically. "A whole
mob of men from the glassworks came up Dock Lane
yelling and shouting and waving iron rods. They were
after Mr. Jarves. Can you imagine anything so terrible?"

Ben choked. It was a minute before he could catch his
breath.

"What did they want Mr. Jarves for?" he inquired.

"They were yelling something about a machine. And
no food for their starving babes. It sounded silly to me
because you know how fat some of those factory children
are!"

"Sandwich was a law-abiding town until those foreign
glassworkers came here," sputtered Grandfather.

"Billy Stetson said the mob had been looking for two
other men but had lost them, so they came to get Mr.
Jarves." Phoebe rolled her eyes.

"What did the men do?" asked Ben.

"Stood around for a while, calling to Mr. Jarves to come out and face up to them. They were waving their arms and swearing."

"Did Mr. Jarves come out?"

"Of course not. Do you think he wanted to get killed? The house was as quiet as anything. You'd think nobody was at home, but a little while earlier I'd seen Mr. Jarves get out of his carriage *in his shirt sleeves* and go in the house. Anna Marie and Jamie couldn't come out and play all day because they had colds, so they were inside, too. They must have been really scared."

Ben took a long swallow of milk. "Did the mob go away?"

"Most of them did, but three men went around to the back of the house and sat down on the porch steps, and three others kept walking up and down in front of the house. The poor Jarves family. They might as well be in prison."

"Phoebe, dear, it sounds to me as if you're exaggerating again," Ma said. "Probably some of those men had been drinking. As soon as they sober up they'll probably apologize to Mr. Jarves and go back to work. How I pity their wives and children."

"No, Ma, I'm not exaggerating." Phoebe was close to tears. "You should have seen them. It was—it was— terrifying!"

Ben opened his mouth to give her some support. Just in time he closed it. How could he ever explain his part in the afternoon's events?

The next day dawned clear and bright. By midmorning the fields were dry, and Ben and Grandfather worked at the haying. As they headed toward the house at noontime Ben glimpsed a vessel beating its way toward shore. There was no mistaking its sturdy hull and patched sails.

"The *Orion!* She's coming in!" he shouted, and ran to tell Ma.

Instantly the house was in a hubbub. In an hour, two at the most, Captain Cyrus Tate would be at home. The noon meal was hastily eaten. Phoebe was dispatched to fetch eggs for custard and a festive cake, then to tell Honor of the *Orion*'s coming. Ma began stirring and mixing, her eyes shining with the special look she always had when Pa's schooner was sighted. Grandfather went to the garden to pick peas, and Ben, stuffing a cherry tart into his mouth, started for the creek. He had more than enough time to row to the town wharf, but he knew his mother would not give him a moment's peace until he set out.

At Ira's shop Ben halted. The door was open, and for a minute he thought Ira was not there. Then he spied him sitting in an old chair in a cobwebby corner, his head sunk in his hands. At Ben's greeting he looked up.

"Oh, hello, Ben," he said listlessly.

"Guess you're pretty tired today, eh?" asked Ben.

"I am." Ira's voice was as dull as his face.

"Pa's schooner is coming in," added Ben. "I'm on my way to meet it."

"That's good." The words were flat.

Ben looked at his friend in consternation. Ira was usually so cheerful and energetic. He didn't seem like the same man today. Yesterday must have taken more out of him than Ben had realized.

Ben said good-by and left. He'd been going to tell Ira how the men had gone after Mr. Jarves yesterday, but such news might sink Ira further into gloom.

Rowing down the creek, Ben looked back over his shoulder from time to time at the *Orion* as she sailed into the harbor's mouth on the incoming tide. She was riding high in the water, a sure sign of a skimpy cargo.

The sun was warm on his back as he bent to the oars, pulling against the current. The air was crisp and salt-laden; puffy white clouds sailed in a brilliant blue sky. On the other side of the marsh a black smudge of smoke rose from the factory chimneys. Ben turned his head so that he would not have to look at the glassworks, but he could not so easily turn his thoughts away from yesterday's trouble. Perhaps he could talk to Pa about it.

He had tied up the skiff and was standing on the wharf when the *Orion* sailed alongside. He caught the stern line and spread its stiff loop over a bollard, then ran across the echoing boards to catch and make fast the line from the bow.

Pa stood at the wheel, one hand raised in greeting. He was squarely built, taller than Grandfather, and a bit shorter than Ben. His strong, even features were ruddy from sun and wind, his dark hair streaked with gray. When he was on the *Orion,* he was all business.

"All well at home, Ben?" he asked briefly. At Ben's assent, he began to give orders. Some of the cargo was to be unloaded immediately. The rest could wait until tomorrow.

Caleb Wilcox greeted Ben warmly. "How's Honor—
and Noah?" he asked. The smile in his long thin face
was anxious. His teeth were strong and white in his
tanned face, and his hair was bleached to the color of
straw. It was clear that he could hardly wait to be off the
schooner and on his way to the small white cottage. He
fumbled with the hatch cover and dropped bales of
cloth in his excitement. The four crew members joked
at each mishap.

"Watch out, Caleb, or you'll be dropping the baby
the same way."

"If you can't work any better than that, Honor won't
want you around the house."

With each laughing remark Caleb grew more flus-
tered.

Finally Captain Tate called out, "That will do for
today. Make her ready for the night, and you can go
home."

The work was finished in short order and within a
few minutes the crew had left. Caleb and the captain
placed their gear in the skiff and stepped in. Ben, at the
oars, was glad for the tide that flowed smoothly up the
creek, bearing the boat along with it. Although heavily
laden, it was easy to row, and he made rapid and steady
progress.

Caleb did not wait until the skiff was tied up. He set
off swiftly down the road toward his home. Pa was almost as bad. He whistled impatiently through his teeth
while Ben laid the oars under the thwarts, then led the
way toward the homestead. This was no time to tell Pa

about Ira's pressing machine, Ben realized. He shouldered the heavy canvas bag and followed.

As they neared the house Ma came out the door, her cheeks as pink as a girl's, walked straight into the captain's arms, and with a long sigh laid her head on his shoulder.

Now the days flew by in a whirl of activity. There was the rest of the cargo to unload—superfine flour and stoves from Philadelphia, umbrellas and knives from New York, and crockery from Newport. The hay had to be cut, spread, dried, raked, and hauled to the mow in the barn.

The corn ripened, the beans grew apace, the squash rounded out, and Ben wished he were triplets, there was so much work to be done. Pa helped in the fields and gardens for a week or two, but he went daily to the *Orion*. Caleb stayed aboard during the daytime, ready to take orders for the next cargo. But only a few men spoke for space in the hold.

One morning Captain Tate announced, "Guess I'll have to make my own cargo. 'Twon't be the first time. Hitch up the team, Ben, and we'll take a load of those logs you and I cut last winter down to the sawmill. Lumber fetches a good price in Philadelphia."

Ben was so busy between farm and wood lot, mill and schooner, he had no time to go into the village. Phoebe brought news from her visits to the Stetson house.

"Those men are still waiting around for Mr. Jarves. He hasn't come out yet!" she announced one night at supper. "He's been inside a whole month."

Ben felt a chill of apprehension. The glassworkers were showing more than a quick flare of temper. Their hostility must be deep-seated and serious. For the hundredth time he thanked his lucky stars that he and Ira had escaped from the mob.

"That's a shocking situation in this day and age," said Ma. She looked toward the men. "Can't the town do something about it?"

Grandfather shrugged. "Why should it?" he asked. "This is a matter between Jarves and his men. Let him settle it."

Ma served fresh peach shortcake and passed a pitcher of heavy cream to pour over it.

"Abba Stetson asked me today, Pa, why you don't carry glass goods on the *Orion*," said Phoebe. "Her father is going to have a new shed built to store the glass in. He can't get it shipped out fast enough, she says." Phoebe dipped into her shortcake importantly, proud of her friendship with the daughter of the factory's superintendent.

"It seems to me you know a lot about the glass business nowadays," said Captain Tate. "Will Stetson's got a pretty important job, I'd say. I wonder how he likes working for his brother-in-law." Pa had known Captain Will Stetson when he was a seafaring man, before his sister Anna had become Mrs. Deming Jarves.

"I suppose there's no harm in keeping the business in the family," commented Ma evenly.

"You didn't answer my question, Pa," Phoebe said pertly.

"Well, I've nothing against Deming Jarves. But I was

one of the few who voted against the glassworks' being built here. Guess I just liked the town the way it was. And having voted against the factory, I don't like to ask for their business."

"Even if you're having a hard time getting a cargo?" asked Phoebe.

The captain smiled. "Not such a hard time," he said equably. "Another week and the *Orion's* hold will be full of first-class lumber. Now you stop worrying about my business and let me attend to it."

At the end of the week Ben helped load the last boards on the schooner. His father followed him off the vessel and paused beside the wagon.

"I'm staying aboard tonight," he said. "We'll be going out with the tide, at dawn. Take care of things at home, Son. Your mother and I depend on you."

Ben listened in amazement. Pa was talking to him as if he were a grown man. He struggled for words but could find none except, "I'll try, Pa."

Then the captain leaped across the space between the wharf and deck, and Ben picked up the reins. All the way home he wished that he had told Pa about the pressing machine. He had wanted to, but they had both been so busy that the time had never seemed right.

The Fugitive

Just as dusk was falling, Ben pulled into the barn and he was about to unharness the team when his mother came into the dim stable, a lantern in one hand, and a bundle over her other arm.

"Your father forgot his warm coat. He hasn't needed it ashore, but he will as soon as he gets out to sea." Carefully she set the lantern on a shelf.

Ben was tired after a long day's work. Besides, he had hoped to pay Ira a visit tonight.

"Hasn't Pa got another coat on board?"

"No, that one was torn, and he brought it ashore for me to mend. I have them both here. I'm sorry, but I'll have to ask you to take them to him."

Ben gritted his teeth. He was sick and tired of making trips to the *Orion*. His backside ached from jolting over rutted roads on the hard seat of the farm wagon. "I'll take the skiff," he said. "It will be a change."

"Good," said Ma. "I'll help you unharness."

Together they unhooked the traces from the whiffle-tree and threw them over the horses' backs. Ben unbuckled the heavy collars, removed the breeching, and hung the harness on the wooden wall pegs. Then Ma unfastened the bridles, and both horses had a long drink of water.

"I'll give them their oats," she offered, starting to fill the measure. There was plenty of hay in the mangers, Ben knew.

When he stepped outside, the two coats over his arm, the yard was in darkness. There was no moon; only a few stars winked overhead.

"Do you need the lantern, Ben?" his mother called.

"No, thanks, I know the way without it."

Then he was down the path to the road, and along it to the bend in the creek. He set the coats in the skiff, jerked the half hitch open, fished out the oars, and shoved out into the water.

Gliding through the blackness was eerie. There was no sound but the creak of the oars against the tholes, the swish of the blades, and the drip of falling drops. His eyes grew accustomed to the blackness. He could see the outline of the grass-covered banks and the ghostly sweep of distant dunes.

Faint shouts came through the quiet evening. At a spot where the marsh curved toward the village center, he saw moving lights. Soon more lights joined the earlier ones; they spread out in a line and moved across the marsh toward the creek.

Why were people searching in the marsh tonight? Had a child been lost? Had a cow or sheep wandered off and got caught in the mire? Had someone broken a leg in a salt hole?

The lights drew nearer. Ben could see that they were torches borne by men. Now and then two or three would draw together at a clump of bushes. What were they after?

Ben had just lifted his oars on a backward swing when a dark shape rose from the creek bank, a hand gripped the gunwale, slowing the boat, and a low voice said, "Take me out to that schooner by the wharf. I'll pay any price you ask."

Ben almost fell over backward; his oars threw up a shower of spray.

"Who are you?" he gasped.

"Never mind," said the man. "Just take me to that schooner. It's a matter of life and death." He crawled over the side and crouched in the skiff.

There was no mistaking that imperious tone. No one but Deming Jarves spoke in quite that way. He must have eluded the guards at the rear of his house and hidden in the marsh.

Ben started to row again, setting the oars into the water at a precise angle, feathering them neatly so that no telltale splash might betray their presence. As his arms worked, his mind did also. The men on the marsh were glassworkers looking for Mr. Jarves. There was no telling how violent they would become if they found him. And if they discovered Ben with Mr. Jarves, they would be sure Ben was associated with the older man in a plot to deprive them of their jobs. He had to save not only Mr. Jarves but himself as well.

The creek wound through the marsh. Just ahead it swung in a wide arc back toward the village. There was no other way to go, nothing to do but keep rowing. The torches came closer.

Dip the oars, pull, lift, swing ever so softly just over the surface. Ben kept his arms moving in steady rhythm, his weariness forgotten as he watched the oncoming searchers.

"Lie down in the bottom of the boat and pull those coats over you," he said to Mr. Jarves. He kept his voice as soft as possible.

There was a faint splash and a barely audible grunt. He'd forgotten to bail out the skiff. Mr. Jarves shouldn't mind a little wetting. It was better than getting killed.

Now the skiff was drawing abreast of the line of hunters. They were from the glassworks, no doubt about it; he recognized two of them. Tucking his chin low into his shirt collar, Ben kept to the far side of the creek and continued his steady pulling. Dip, pull, lift, swing. Dip, pull—.

"Hi, there. Where be ye going this time o' night?" A burly man hailed him.

"To my Pa's schooner. He forgot his coats, and I'm taking them out to him." Ben tried to keep his voice steady. His stomach was a hard knot, and he was short of breath.

"That's a fine story. Why didn't ye wait till mornin'?"

"Because he's sailing with the tide, at first light." While he spoke, Ben kept on rowing. The man walked along the bank, torch aloft, swinging it toward Ben.

"How do I know those are coats?" he growled suspiciously.

"Look." Swiftly Ben bent forward, and still holding

the oars with one hand, he used the other to lift one of the coat sleeves that lay loose on the humped bundle at his feet, and flapped it back and forth.

"All right. Get on wi' ye. But keep yer eyes peeled for a man. Maybe ye know him. Old Jarves. We're after him, and we'll get him, that we will." The man rejoined his fellows.

Ben swung his oars faster. Noise didn't matter now. All that counted was speed. One of the other searchers might have the sense to look beneath the coats. He had just pulled the skiff out of the circle of light when, as he had expected, a man ran toward the bank and called out, "Hey, you. Come back here and let us look in your boat."

Ben made no answer but pulled with as much strength as he could for the harbor and the town wharf. The creek had never seemed so long, nor the skiff so slow. At last the creek bed widened, and he entered the broad, deep waters at the town wharf.

The *Orion* was dark except for her riding lights, and one small glow in the cabin. Ben pulled the skiff between the pilings, under the wharf, and made the painter fast. He felt in the darkness for the ladder he knew was there. His fingers closed around the slippery boards. There was a rustle as Mr. Jarves threw the coats aside.

"You'd better stay here," said Ben, "while I go and talk with my father."

Then he was up the ladder, across the shadowy wharf, and on board the *Orion*. Pa must have ears like a fox.

He was waiting at the companionway when Ben's feet touched the deck.

"It's me, Pa," said Ben, very low. "Can I talk to you in the cabin?" He waited for his father to go down first, then ducked his head and followed.

The small cubicle was bare and tidy, the berths on two sides smooth, the small iron stove still warm. Some charts were spread out on the center table.

"What is it, Son? Are you in trouble?"

Ben explained about Mr. Jarves. His father nodded. "I saw the lights. Looks like the Carolinas when a fugitive slave is being hunted. The only thing missing was the bay of bloodhounds. Tell me the whole story, Son."

When he was through, Ben felt great relief. It was good to share his anxiety. Some day he would ask his father if it was right to make machines that might cause hardship to some folks. Right now there was the problem of Mr. Jarves.

"I guess we'll have to bring him aboard," Pa said. "They're sure to find him if he stays in the skiff. By the time it's daylight we'll be on our way to Philadelphia and he'll be safe."

Together they went up on deck. "You give him the word," said Pa. "I'll keep watch here."

Ben crept across the wharf, lay down on the edge, and poked his head over the side. "You can come up now," he said. "Would you please hand up the coats first."

He felt rough wool beneath his fingers and drew the garments onto the wharf, then waited for Deming Jarves to climb the ladder. For a city man Mr. Jarves

was pretty spry. In no time at all they were in the
Orion's cabin.

Ben blinked at the tall man before him. Six weeks
indoors had given Mr. Jarves a sickly pallor. His flight
across the marsh had removed any trace of elegance. His
fair hair lay in a tangle across his brow, his face was
scratched and smirched, and the suit that had been so
fine was now torn and wet, stained with green slime and
mud. But he still seemed to feel himself in command.

"I'm grateful to you for taking me aboard, Captain
Tate," he said. "I remember you from town meeting.
My chief concern, now that you have helped me to
elude those ruffians, is to get to Boston as soon as possible."

Cyrus Tate ran a bronzed hand through his hair. "I'd
like to accommodate you, Mr. Jarves," he said, "but the
truth is that I'm sailing for Philadelphia with a load of
lumber."

"I'm sure you could find a market for it in Boston just
as well," said Mr. Jarves easily.

"I could find a market all right, but for less money. So
much timber is coming down the Middlesex Canal from
New Hampshire these days that the price has gone way
down in Boston. I cannot afford to sell my lumber for so
little." Cyrus Tate set his jaw.

"That's easily taken care of. I'll pay you the difference. And give you, say, one hundred dollars to boot."
Deming Jarves tilted his head to one side in a confident
manner.

Captain Tate's face flushed. He coughed and looked
at a point above the other man's head. "I'm not so sure

that I want to go to Boston. I had my mind set on Philadelphia."

"Five hundred dollars, then."

The captain's face took on an even deeper hue. He
regarded Deming Jarves with exasperation. "Don't you
know you can't buy every man in Sandwich?"

The other laughed shortly. "Don't I? Have you forgotten those glassworkers out there in the marsh?"

Ben's head was spinning. If Pa and Mr. Jarves wanted
to argue, let them. "I'll be going now," he said, and
started for the companionway.

"Just a minute." Mr. Jarves put a restraining hand on
his arm. "Those men are out for blood tonight. I
wouldn't want it to be yours."

"I'll be all right," said Ben impatiently. He'd got
through once, he could do it again. As he spoke, doubt
began to seep into his mind. Would the men recognize
him on the way back?

His father's words echoed his thoughts. "You're right,
Jarves. They'll be looking for Ben, now, too."

Ben looked from his father's sternly set jaw to Mr.
Jarves's firm mouth. He might try to oppose one.
Against both he'd never win. He sank down on the edge
of his father's berth.

The two men were eyeing each other. The captain
spoke first. "Very well, Jarves, I'll take you to Boston.
And I'll accept the difference in the price of the lumber.
But that's all. You must understand that it wasn't
money that swayed me, but your concern for my son's
safety."

The captain's voice was fading. Ben leaned on one

elbow and lifted his feet onto the gray blanket. The berth felt unbelievably comfortable.

"I wish that my boy—" Mr. Jarves began. Ben never heard what it was he wished, for the man's voice receded further and further into the distance, and was finally lost altogether.

When Ben awoke, the schooner was pitching violently. Gray light showed at the portholes. He lifted his head and looked across the cabin to the other berth. There lay Deming Jarves, his long body braced against the sideboards, his eyes just opening.

Ben sat up, his stomach churning. "We're at sea," he exclaimed. "I'd thought to go home before we sailed." He clenched his fist in anger. Now he was in for another bout of seasickness. What could be worse?

"The men were still searching the marsh this morning, and we feared you might not get across it safely," said the man. "Your father sent a message to your mother to let her know you're safe." He gave Ben a keen glance. "Don't tell me the son of a sea captain falls prey to *mal de mer*."

"If you mean do I get seasick, you're right," said Ben. "Pa says he never saw anybody so bad." He looked across at Mr. Jarves and saw that the skin around his mouth had a greenish tinge. "Aren't you a good sailor, either?"

"I ought to be, after all the times I've crossed the Atlantic," said Mr. Jarves bitterly, "but every time a ship starts rolling—well, you understand."

For a moment they were both quiet. Then Mr. Jarves said briskly, "Only one thing helps. Put your mind on something so interesting that you can forget your stomach. Now then, Ben, what are you most excited about in all the world?"

Ben lay silent. No one had ever asked him that.

"What do you want to be when you're a man? A sailor like your father?" Deming Jarves laughed shortly. "No, I guess not. Well, then, do you want to farm? Or go into some profession? Doctor? Lawyer?"

"I'm not sure," said Ben, swallowing hard against his growing queasiness. "Most of all I like to fix things like pumps and clocks, and figure out new ways to do things. Our cow Narcissa was going to be put out of the way because some men from the glass factory shot her in the leg." He gulped and paused. For a minute he had forgotten that he was talking to the head of the glassworks.

"On purpose?" demanded Mr. Jarves.

"No, it was an accident. They'd been drinking."

"Liquor seems to go with glassmaking," Mr. Jarves said regretfully. "It's the curse of the business. What did you do about the cow?"

Ben explained about the sling and the special platform and said that Narcissa was making steady improvement during her enforced rest and was growing sleek and fat. Mr. Jarves chuckled when Ben told about going to milk her one evening and finding her with all four hoofs off the floor, swaying gently and contentedly.

Rain slatted against the portholes, and the schooner rolled from side to side. Ben could feel his stomach rolling, too.

"What other ideas have you had?" asked Mr. Jarves.

"I helped Ira with the pressing machine. You see, I'd

been working on my sister's pump. And that gave me a clue to a handle for the press."

"It was a good idea," said Deming Jarves warmly.

"It only brought trouble, though," said Ben. "You were like a prisoner for six weeks, and the machine was smashed to bits. It can never be repaired."

"The machine may have been destroyed, but the idea is just as good as ever. Benson can build another," said the man confidently.

Ben sighed. "I'm afraid Ira won't do it. He's all upset. He thought his machine was going to help people by making glassware with less time and labor, but instead it might put the glassworkers out of their jobs."

Mr. Jarves sat up so quickly that he bumped his head on the berth above. He did not seem to notice, but swung his feet over the side and leaned forward, striking one hand against the other in emphasis.

"That's not true. There will always be work for skilled glass blowers. The pressing machine will create new jobs for more workers. Its product will not be in competition with hand-blown ware. Pressed glass will be so easy to make and so low in price that every family will be able to afford glass tumblers and plates."

"Do you really think so, Mr. Jarves?" In his eagerness Ben sat up.

"Most certainly. The machine you helped build pressed only one article at a time. Why couldn't one be made that would produce six or a dozen at once?"

"Why didn't you tell the glass blowers this?" asked Ben.

"I tried to that afternoon in the glasshouse. But they wouldn't listen."

"If they had listened to you, they'd understand there was nothing to fear from the machine."

Mr. Jarves shook his head sadly. "Ignorance is the worst enemy of progress. An early steamboat was torn to pieces by angry boatmen. A mill containing early power looms was burned by suspicious weavers."

"There must be some way to let the men know the presssing machine won't take their jobs away from them," Ben pursued.

"They'll find out in time. I'll write to Benson and ask him to build another. When I return we can make further improvements."

"Are you really coming back to Sandwich? After the way the men acted?"

"You don't think I'd let a mob keep me from my business? Hostile crowds are no novelty in my family. My grandmother was a Seabury. She often told me how, when she was a girl, a mob came after her uncle Samuel Seabury, and he had to go into hiding."

"Did he escape?" asked Ben.

"He not only escaped, but he became the first Episcopal bishop in the United States. Surely you've heard of him."

"No," said Ben. He was beginning to realize that there was a lot he didn't know.

For a few minutes there was silence. The tossing of the ship continued. Mr. Jarves lay back on his berth, and Ben did the same. He could feel the sweat breaking out on his forehead. In a few minutes—

A shaky voice came from the other berth. "You've told me what you like best to do, Ben. Let me tell you what I'm most interested in. Glass! There's nothing in the world quite so fascinating! What do you know about glass, Ben?"

"Just what I saw that day in the glasshouse." How much longer before he had to give in to the growing sickness?

"Not many people know about the romance in glass, Ben. It was discovered centuries ago, history says, by a band of Phoenicians who built their evening fire on some cakes of soda set in the sand. In the morning they found a hard, shiny, brittle substance where the heat had fused the two. From this beginning men went on to make beautiful glassware, heavy and substantial at first, then more delicate and fragile. Have you ever seen Venetian glass?"

"There's a vase in the tavern, on the parlor mantelpiece."

"Yes, that's Venetian. The glassmakers in Venice formed guilds. They surrounded the craft with mystery and told tales of a salamander or dragon in the glass furnace. The knights of old who attacked the salamander were vanquished, probably because their metal armor conducted the fierce heats. You know how metal gets hot near a fire."

Was Ben imagining it, or was the schooner heaving in a less sickening fashion?

"I don't see how the men stand the heat in the glasshouse," he said.

"You ought to be there when they're replacing a pot.

The heat is really fierce, then," said Mr. Jarves. "In the old days the workmen used to wrap the skins of wild animals around themselves, with the fur on the outside, as protection. Afterward they would parade through the village, and the townsfolk would think they were strange gods and run away in terror."

"If the work is so dangerous, why do men keep at it?"

"There's a mystery and romance about glass that fascinate men. And there's a challenge, too, to make finer, clearer glass and brighter colors. Did you know glass can be made in scores of colors—rich amethyst-purple, deep sapphire-blue, and topaz-gold? We can make all those at Sandwich, and many more. I've mixed and tested and changed my formulas until we can turn out colors as beautiful as any in the world."

Mr. Jarves's brow wrinkled. "There's one colored glass I'd give anything to make—the golden ruby. It was discovered over a hundred years ago by Johann Kunckel. Now only the Bohemians have the secret of its ingredients. You never saw anything so glowing, so warm and rich, yet so clear and beautiful. It's easy to understand why people used to believe that such glass had magical properties, and that drinking from it gave protection from all manner of ills." He sighed. "Perhaps some day—" His cheeks had taken on a faint pink, as if talking about the golden-ruby glass had given him a tinge of its color.

The rain had stopped, and the ship's motion had settled to a steady, rhythmic roll. Thin sunlight filtered through the portholes. Mr. Jarves put out one foot in an exploring fashion. He looked inquiringly at Ben.

"Do you think we could go up on deck? The air would do us good, and I think I might even chew on a dry biscuit."

Ben followed, shaky, but feeling better with each step. If ever he found himself aboard a ship again, he'd remember Mr. Jarves's cure for seasickness. It really worked.

The Steamboat

By the time the *Orion* sailed into Boston Harbor Ben was hungrier than he could remember being in his entire life. Mr. Jarves must have been in the same state, because when he and Pa walked forward to the bow where Caleb was pointing out the sights to Ben, he said, "I'd be pleased if you gentlemen would join me for dinner."

The sun was low in the sky. The dinner hour is long since past, Ben thought, and then he realized that city folk called their evening meal dinner.

Pa said, "Caleb and I have our going-ashore clothes, but Ben has only what he's standing in, not exactly fit garb for a social occasion."

Mr. Jarves laughed, looking down at his stained and rumpled suit. "I'm not exactly the glass of fashion, myself. If you can excuse my appearance, I certainly will his."

The prospect of food was so absorbing that Ben hardly noticed the city. So many ships were moored in the harbor or tied up at the wharves jutting out from shore that the masts seemed as thick as trees in a forest. Warehouses and sheds lined the wharves. And beyond them, on three hills, rose thickly crowded houses, shops, and buildings. Smoke from hundreds of chimneys clouded the sky.

Once the *Orion* had been berthed and left in the charge of two crew members, they set out through the busy streets, Pa and Mr. Jarves in the lead, Caleb and Ben following. Ben's stomach was so empty he was sure it had plastered itself against his backbone.

Over round cobblestones they walked, their feet slipping in filth. Carts loaded with hogsheads rumbled past, wagons piled high with vegetables jolted by, and men trundled wheelbarrows of coal or firewood at the sides of the streets. An occasional carriage rattled along. In between and on all sides of the moving vehicles were more people than Ben had ever seen in one place before. There were women with bundles under their arms, their long skirts dragging; clerks in high collars and stovepipe hats; stevedores in rough shirts; and everywhere small girls and boys, skipping, running, darting here and there. Noise filled the air: the squeak and rumble of wheels, the low gutturals of men and high cries of children, the whicker or snort of horses, and overhead, the scream of gulls. The smells were as varied—the fishy, salty tang of the harbor, the strong odor of horses and of men's sweating bodies, and the tantalizing fragrance of roasting meats that floated from the doorways of eating places.

Ahead, on Union Street, was a sign—Union Oyster House. As Mr. Jarves turned into the doorway, Ben felt a stab of disappointment. Oysters! Who in the world wanted those? Inside was a broad counter of soapstone where three men with short-bladed knives were opening oysters, which waiters bore away by the plateful as soon as they were ready to the booths that filled the room. Some eager eaters were gathered about the bar, downing the juicy oysters straight from the shell.

Ben followed the others to a booth. If Mr. Jarves thought he was doing him a favor buying him oysters, he was mistaken. He'd like some real food. When a waiter put a menu in front of him, Ben's glance went no farther than *roast beef.* He knew at once what his choice would be.

"Will you have a drink, sir?" Mr. Jarves invited.

"Thank you, no," the captain replied. "Cold water is good enough."

"A little wine perhaps?"

"Nothing at all. I've seen too much sorrow brought on by drink." Pa's voice was pleasant but firm.

"I wish my workmen were of the same opinion," said Mr. Jarves.

When they had all eaten their fill, they walked outside into the twilight. Ben looked around curiously. The crowds had thinned, and now that he was no longer half-starved he could put his mind on the sights.

A short distance away he saw what appeared to be a long, narrow vessel moving slowly along, drawn by two horses at the end of a long rope. He rubbed his eyes. The harbor was some distance away. What was a boat doing in the middle of the city?

"That's a branch of the Middlesex, the canal that

connects the Merrimack River with the Charles," said Mr. Jarves. "When the canal was first built, goods had to be carted from Boston to the canal terminus in Charlestown by way of the bridge over the Charles River. Then somebody figured out a way to get canal barges across the river to Boston by means of a sunken cable with floats attached. The bargemen haul up the cable and pull their craft across to enter the canal to Haymarket Square, handy to the public market."

He broke off, for above the noise of creaking wheels and clattering hoofs came another sound, a long drawn-out toot, a mournful wail such as Ben had never heard before.

Mr. Jarves said in excitement, "That must be the *Patent* arriving from Portland! Would you like to watch her come in to the wharf?"

Would he? Ben stood on his toes, craning his neck in the direction from which the blast of steam had come. He'd never thought he'd be lucky enough to see a vessel driven by a steam engine. He hurried after the men.

When they gained the wharf and a clear view of the approaching vessel, Ben blinked in disbelief. Instead of masts, a tall stack rose from the deck, spouting black smoke and sparks. A tremendous noise accompanied its progress, a monstrous puffing, punctuated by a clank and rasp of metal, and muffled splashes. Behind foamed a double wake. Ben watched in wonder as the ship moved steadily along, threading its way through the crowded harbor to the wharf. To his further amazement, it moved directly toward the pier against the receding tide, without tacking.

"I've seen such vessels in New York," said Cyrus Tate. "Don't know as I'd have much faith in them."

"Steam will be the motive power of the future," said Deming Jarves, "on land as well as sea. Would you like to go aboard the *Patent?* I've some acquaintance with the vessel's owner."

Ben gave his arm a hard pinch. Could this be happening to him? His feet scarcely touching the gangplank, he trailed after the men as they made their way among the disembarking passengers to the ship's deck.

For the next half hour Ben's mind worked at top speed. The captain considered the steamboat the greatest invention of the century. He was more than pleased to explain its workings.

Standing beside a pile of wood, he pointed to a furnace, its doors warped by heat. "A man has to work full time feeding wood into it to keep the steam up in the boiler," he said, gesturing to a large rectangular tank above the furnace. "The steam goes through a pipe to the cylinder, where its pressure drives the piston."

"The engine utilizes the expansive force of steam," Mr. Jarves explained to Ben. "The piston fits snugly inside the cylinder, and by means of a connecting rod, drives the crank shaft." He indicated the various parts of machinery.

"The shaft turns the paddle wheels," the captain went on. "Of course, they rotate more slowly than the crank shaft, and have to be geared down. We're having trouble with the gears. The last set were brittle, and the teeth wouldn't stand the pressure. I'll lay over tomorrow and replace them if the new set has arrived from the ironworks."

Ben peered at the cylinder and at the top of the piston with its protruding rod. How he longed to see the engine operating. He would have liked to stay on board all night, learning more, but the captain was looking at his watch.

"Sorry to hurry you gentlemen, but I must find out if the new gears have arrived."

All too soon they were back on the wharf. As they were making their way toward the *Orion,* a heavy dray thundered past, its driver urging the four-horse team to get a move on. From beneath the canvas-covered load dripped a trickle of water. Ben felt a chill as the wagon passed by.

"That's one of Frederic Tudor's wagons," Mr. Jarves said. "He cuts ice from ponds in Saugus, stores it in his icehouses, and ships it to the West Indies, where he gets twenty-five cents a pound for it. He's made such a fortune he's called the Ice King."

"That much a pound? He must make a mighty profit!" exclaimed Caleb. "Why don't we try something like that, Captain?"

"I've thought of it," said Cyrus. "Suppose you were becalmed in the tropics? What would become of your cargo?"

"I've a better proposition for you than ice," said Deming Jarves. "I've got more glass in my warehouse than I have vessels to ship it in. What I need is responsible men like yourself whom I can trust. Right now there's a shipment of glass due in Philadelphia, and a cargo of special sand to be brought back from New Jersey. Our Cambridge factory prepares all the red lead for the Sandwich plant. I dare say there's a quantity waiting now to go to Sandwich that you could take on your return trip. Now here are my terms." He lowered his voice and continued to talk. Discussion followed, then Deming Jarves put out his hand and said, "Is it agreed?"

The captain took the proffered hand and shook it solemnly, saying, "Agreed." It had all happened so naturally that Ben did not even wonder at the dissolution of his father's former opposition.

Ben dreamed that night of taking a shipload of ice to the Indies in a vessel powered by steam. All night long he heaved wood into the great boiler, watched pistons and valves, and checked the steam gauge.

The next morning he was so preoccupied that his father said, "I don't need you, Ben, to help unload. Would you like to look around the city some more?"

There was just one place Ben wanted to go. Back to the steamboat. The captain had said he had to repair the engine. Perhaps he'd be willing to answer some questions.

The steamboat wharf was deserted except for an elderly man shaking his fist at a sign that read: *Patent* schedule delayed one day. Ben ducked under a rope and walked boldly across the gangplank. The deck was empty, but from below came a loud clanging. He found the captain working alone.

At the sight of Ben he exclaimed, "I hoped you were my mate. He's sick today, of all times." He struck with a hammer at a cogged wheel. "I can't seem to get this free. It's rusted on."

Ben examined the gear. It was made in two parts that fitted over the shaft, and was held together by bolts and nuts. "Want me to hold the bolt fast while you heave on the nut?" asked Ben.

The man nodded, and fitted a wrench over the nut while Ben held the head of the bolt with another wrench. The next minute he could feel the wrench twisting in his hands. With all his force he held it firm while the man grunted and strained.

Suddenly the man cried triumphantly, "Got it!" and unscrewed the nut. "Now let's tackle the other."

An hour flew by. Between them, Ben and the captain got the old gears off the shaft and fitted on the new ones. They were a bit tight, and the shaft had to be filed down. Then the captain went over every section of the engine, checking it for wear and oiling each movable part. As he worked, he talked, and soon Ben felt that he knew the steam engine as well as he knew Honor's pump.

When they were finished, the captain put his hand in his pocket. "How much do I owe you?" he asked.

"Not a thing," said Ben. "I was glad to learn more about the engine."

"I must say your questions had more sense than most. One man asked me why we had paddle wheels on both sides. Thought one would be easier to run." The captain threw back his head and laughed.

For a minute Ben looked at him questioningly. Then

he, too, saw the joke. With a paddle wheel on just one side the ship would go round and round in a circle.

He was leaving when the captain said, "Any time you're looking for a job, come and see me. I could use a young fellow that catches on as quick as you."

The Orion's Departure

A job on a steamboat! Ben couldn't imagine anything more exciting. In a daze he walked back to the *Orion,* his head whirling.

His head was whirling, but in a different way the next day as he stood on the deck of the schooner, homeward bound. The vessel scudded briskly along in a fresh breeze. There was sunshine and a bright blue sky with little wisps of white cloud traced upon it. Ben would have been completely happy but for the rise and fall of the ship. Each time the bow rose, his stomach rose with it. Each time it fell, so did his insides. He'd mastered this weakness when he was with Mr. Jarves. Why couldn't he now?

Caleb came up to him. "That was quite a puffer of a steamboat."

"The captain says they'll put sailing ships out of business someday," said Ben.

"Put sails out of business! Impossible!" sputtered Caleb.

"He said there's a steam engine on wheels that will do the work of horses," Ben continued.

"That's a good one," laughed Caleb. "Nothing could ever take the place of horses."

When the cook beat with an iron spoon on a pan as a signal that dinner was ready, Ben was more than hungry for the fish and potatoes. By four o'clock they had sighted the Sandwich dunes and the opening where the creek wound in toward the village.

"I'd like to see a steamboat make any better time than we did today," said Captain Tate proudly.

By six o'clock they were home again. Ben was thankful that Pa was there to explain to Ma and Grandfather why he hadn't returned from his evening's errand to the *Orion*. Had it been only three nights ago? It seemed more like three years, so much had happened in the meantime.

At supper, after warning Phoebe not to breathe a word to anyone about how Mr. Jarves had escaped, Pa told about his arrangement to carry shipments for the Boston and Sandwich Glass Company. Grandfather listened in shocked silence, then scowled fiercely and made a sound of disgust deep in his throat.

"To think my own son would be a turncoat, playing into the hands of the man who's bringing evil and destruction upon us all."

"If you could meet Mr. Jarves and talk with him, you'd understand he's not a bad sort," said Captain Tate. "It's not his fault his workmen carouse around and set off firearms. He'd much rather they'd stay sober and stick to their jobs. Most of them don't know what it is to own property. He's letting them pay so much a month for their houses. He wants them to settle down and be content." As an afterthought he added, "Mr. Jarves offered to buy us another cow, but I told him Narcissa would be all right."

Grandfather would not be mollified. "It's one thing to pay for a cow. It's another to ruin an entire town." He stamped from the table, chewing at his white mustache.

The rest of the family was happy about the decision.

"If you must be at sea, Cyrus, it's good to know you'll always have a cargo ready," said Ma.

"Now I can tell Abba Stetson that my father works for the glass company, too," said Phoebe, tossing her head.

Ben wondered if she noticed the clouding of Pa's eyes. But all the captain said was, "After this voyage I can pay the taxes and get a new set of sails."

When Ben went out to see Narcissa she bent her head toward his and thrust her dripping tongue out at him. He ducked, and patted her cheek. "How's your leg coming along?" he asked.

As if in answer, Narcissa moved her injured limb, trying to stretch it downward to find secure footing. He could swear she was smiling at him.

The next morning Dr. Dow came. "I just stopped by to see my patient," he explained as he got out of his buggy and pulled up his coat collar against the thin rain.

Ma came out of the kitchen with an apron thrown over her head, Phoebe at her heels, squealing in the wet.

Ben threw a forkful of salt hay into the freshly cleaned horse stall and leaned the fork against the wall.

Dr. Dow circled warily around Narcissa. "Are you sure she won't kick?" he asked nervously.

"If it will make you any easier in your mind, we'll all hold her," said Ma, "but I think you're just putting on a show for us."

He grinned at her. "Hang it all, Margaret, I have to get a little fun out of my job, now that my own life is so empty."

Ma gave him a long look. "You ought to think about marrying again, Justin."

He gave her a wry smile. "All the pretty girls like you are already spoken for."

He leaned over and felt Narcissa's leg. "Can't tell much until we take off the splints." Deftly he unwound the bandages and removed the two narrow strips of wood. Except for a purple scar, the leg looked normal. His strong thin fingers ran up and down its length.

"The bones have knit better than I expected. I doubt, though, that they're strong enough yet to bear her weight as she lies down and gets up. Why don't you take away the platform and lower the sling so that all her feet will touch the floor. Then once or twice a day you could ease her down in the sling so she could lie down."

"I'll stay out here and take care of Narcissa," Phoebe volunteered.

Ben looked at her pityingly. Did she think she was strong enough to haul a cow up by a block and tackle?

"You'd better keep at your sampler," advised Ma. "Aunt Lettie will be here soon for her autumn visit, and she will be looking at your needlework. She sets great store by such things, you know."

"I know," Phoebe said with a groan. "Didn't I have to take out a whole tree last time she came just because the crosses didn't all go the same way?"

The doctor was climbing back into his buggy. "I'll stop by in a few days," he said, then picked up the reins and lifted one hand in farewell.

All that day Pa superintended the loading of the *Orion*. He came in wearily at suppertime, saying, "A cargo of glass is surely different from lumber—in the handling, at least. I've been nervous as a witch for fear the men would start throwing those hogsheads around as if they were filled with apples instead of vases and tumblers. Will Stetson came out with the invoice, and he told me the shipment is worth thousands of dollars. I'm just as glad tomorrow is Sunday."

Tomorrow Sunday! Ben had never known a week to roll around so fast. He thought of church, and wondered if this week he'd catch a glimpse of Emily Griswold. He hadn't seen her since she had let him and Ira hide in the back room of the company store. It was his own fault. He hadn't gone near the factory since that fateful afternoon. And in church he couldn't seem to summon the courage to turn his head during the service and look up at the choir in the balcony at the rear.

The next morning the whole family assembled in their Sunday best. Phoebe had a new blue dress, fluffed out with petticoats, and a blue ribbon in her hair, which was loose across her shoulders, crinkled from a week of tight braids. Ma wore her dark-green bombazine, and

Pa and Grandfather their black suits and high white collars, starched and snowy. Ben's coat was tight across the shoulders; his wrists hung down from the sleeves, and the bottoms of his trousers were a full four inches above his ankles.

"We must get you a new suit," Ma said, "first thing after the taxes. Just try not to take a deep breath."

It was difficult not to breathe deeply of the sweet fresh air sweeping across meadow and marsh as they walked along the road to the center, Ma and Pa in the lead, Grandfather behind them, and Ben and Phoebe at the rear. A song sparrow lilted its melody. Goldenrod and purple asters lined the way. In the hollows sumac lifted scarlet clusters. It was a beautiful day, good for almost anything but being shut up in a stuffy building listening to a long, dull sermon, Ben thought. By the time they reached the millpond, the sun had baked through the wool of Ben's coat. His back felt prickly, and he wished he could dive into the cool water.

Outside the church he looked about for a slight, dark-haired girl. No luck. His parents walked inside; he had no choice but to follow into the family pew, just ahead of the one occupied by Captain Stetson and his family. The Jarves pew was vacant. Mrs. Jarves and the children must have returned to Boston as they always did at the summer's end.

During the long opening prayer Ben had an idea. When the hymn was announced and a rustle from the loft signaled the rising of the choir, he fumbled with his hymnal and let it fall to the floor. As he reached down for it he turned his head up toward the choir loft.

Emily was in the front row looking right at him. Her face turned pink, and she fluttered the fingers of one hand behind her sheet of music. Ben retrieved the hymnal and, just before he straightened up, heard a sharp rip. His coat! From the pew behind came a giggle. Why couldn't that Abba Stetson mind her own business?

The captain's leave-taking the next morning was hurried. Although the tide would not turn until two hours before noon, he wanted to be aboard early to see that his fragile cargo was well secured.

"Don't you worry," he said to Ma. "We should be back home in less than a month." He bent to kiss her, his eyes holding the special look he kept just for her. Then he tweaked Phoebe's pigtails, shook Grandfather's hand, and patted Ben on the shoulder.

The family watched as he walked down the path, sea bag over one shoulder. At the creek one of the crew waited to row him and Caleb to the *Orion*. Soon they were lost to sight in the waving marsh grass.

Ma winked back tears. "No matter how many times I say good-by to Cyrus, I can't help worrying when he goes off."

"No good will come of his carrying goods for that man Jarves," Grandfather said, scowling at the factory's squat bulk and never-ending smoke.

"Don't you think Cyrus is old enough to make his own decisions, Father Tate?" asked Ma with asperity. "Times are changing; we have to move with them."

Grandfather blinked at her. No wonder. Ben couldn't remember Ma ever speaking to Grandfather like that.

"Times may change, but I will not. And Cyrus will regret this day. You'll see that I am right." Grandfather stalked off into the barn, his white beard jutting out portentously.

Beach Plums
and Clams

The first rainy day Ben went to Ira's. To his disappointment the shop was empty, and he had turned to leave when he spied Ira making uneven progress along the road.

As soon as Ira saw Ben, he exclaimed, "Once that letter left my hands I knew that I had made the right decision."

"What are you talking about?" Ben asked.

"Thee knows how troubled I was about the pressing machine and the workmen. Yesterday I had a note from Mr. Jarves asking me to build another machine just like the first. I pondered about it, and asked the Lord for guidance, and the answer came, clear as crystal, that I must say no. The Lord intends me to use my talent to help His people. My machine might bring harm to them instead. So I wrote to Mr. Jarves and told him I would not build another."

For a minute Ben was back in the *Orion*'s damp cabin, lying on his father's berth, listening to Mr. Jarves. If only he could pass on the glass manufacturer's sincere conviction and enthusiasm to Ira! Urging the need for secrecy, Ben told Ira about the manufacturer's escape, and his part in it.

"The pressing machine won't put men out of work, Ira. It will make new jobs for other men. And it will provide lots of glassware at a low price so everybody can have tumblers and lamps and vases—not just rich people."

"Maybe so," admitted Ira, "but it could put the glass blowers out of work if it were perfected."

"Mr. Jarves doesn't think so," said Ben, "and he ought to know. He said every new idea meets with fear and opposition. I wish I could remember all he said."

Ira shook his head stubbornly. "Don't try to change me," he said. "Since I wrote that letter today I've had the first peace in weeks. From now on I'll build things like any other carpenter, that's all."

At the door of the shop Ira paused and gestured for Ben to enter.

Ben couldn't give up. "Do you think it's wrong to work on new ideas? Wouldn't you rig up a sling for Narcissa if she was your cow?"

"I might do that," said Ira. "As a matter of fact, I'm making something now that's a mite different. It's for Noah." He led the way to his workbench and pointed to a high chair. "Most all baby's chairs tip over easily, and their mothers have to watch them all the time. If the babies sit close to the table, they bang on it with spoons or cups and make dents. So here's what I've made. See how the legs go out at an angle? That's to make it steady. I'm going to put a shelf on three sides so there will be a place for toys and a dish. To make sure it won't tip over I'm going to fasten two long hooks under the tray that will fit into two screw eyes underneath the table top. Even Noah, bouncy as he is, can't upset this chair."

"That's wonderful," said Ben. He was tempted to ask if Ira wasn't afraid his high chair would put other carpenters out of work, but he hadn't the heart.

Two weeks later school began. Ben had hoped to see Emily Griswold among the girls and was disappointed that she was not a pupil. She and her father must have moved away. He walked past the factory store and saw a strange man sweeping the steps. That settled it. The Griswolds had left Sandwich. He felt a pang of regret. Emily had practically saved his life, and he had done nothing at all for her in return.

As he was walking back toward town he came face to face with Martin O'Connor. Suddenly Ben realized that Martin had not enrolled in school either. A picture flashed into his mind of Martin throwing an iron rod to trip one of the glassworkers as he was about to strike out at Ben.

"Hello," said Ben, trying to sound friendly.

Martin ducked his head and hurried past.

Ben turned and followed. "Where are you going?" he asked.

"Just out on the marsh." Martin slid a suspicious glance toward Ben.

"Mind if I go along?"

"Makes no difference to me."

They walked in silence until they had left the factory and its cluster of houses behind. Martin led the way across the coarse grass to the edge of the creek, and followed it to the dunes. There he planted his feet in the sand and turned to Ben.

"Well, what do you want?" he demanded.

"To thank you for helping Ira and me get away that day."

"Oh, that," said Martin, his face reddening. "That wasn't anything." He drew in the sand with his bare toe. "Say, how's your cow?"

"She's fine," said Ben heartily.

Martin moved his toe in an intricate design. "I want you to know," he said slowly, "that I wasn't with my uncle and Steve Tully when it happened. I was following them so I could help my uncle home if—if—" He faltered, then went on, "if he got so drunk he couldn't make it alone."

Ben couldn't look at Martin. His misery was too plain.

"Does that happen very often?" he asked.

"Too often," said Martin. "He used to be a gaffer." At Ben's puzzled glance, he explained, "That's the top man in a shop."

"What kind of a shop?" asked Ben.

"Glassworkers have their own lingo," said Martin. "A shop is four men who work together. There's an apprentice, who fetches and carries. That's what I used to be. Then there's a footmaker, who gathers and blows glass, and shapes it on an iron table called a marver. That's what I am now."

"Blowing glass must be something like blowing soap bubbles," Ben offered.

Martin gave him a pitying glance. "It's a little more difficult," he said. "Next is a servitor. He shapes the main body of the object. And finally there's a gaffer, the master glass blower in charge of the shop, who does the final shaping and finishing. That's what my uncle was before he got to drinking so much."

"What does he do now?" asked Ben. Jerry O'Connor was certainly very much in evidence at the factory.

"He fills in when any of the men are out sick, and does odd jobs around the works."

"Does he live with your family?" asked Ben.

"He's all the family I've got," said Martin. He walked toward the water line, where wavelets came and went with a gentle swish.

Ben scuffed along beside him, the water chill on his feet. "You coming back to school?" he inquired.

Martin shook his head. "I can read and write and figure. That's all I need."

"There's a lot more to learn," said Ben.

"All I care about is making glass. School can't help me with that."

"Glass isn't everything," said Ben.

"It is to me," stated Martin firmly. "There's nothing you can't do with glass. I bet that some day there'll be houses made of glass."

Ben had a hard time not laughing. Only Martin's intense earnestness kept him serious.

"When I get to be a gaffer, I'm going to try out some new things," said Martin. "You wait and see."

A cloud covered the sun, bringing a chill to the air.

Ben was suddenly hungry. "Say, Martin, how about coming home with me for supper?" he said.

"Would your mother mind?" asked Martin.

"She'd like it," said Ben.

The next minute Martin's face was as cloudy as the sky. "I can't," he said. "I've got to see that my uncle gets to work."

"Why don't you let him look after himself, just this once?" Ben asked.

Martin gave him a scornful glance. "He's looked out for me since I was six, when my father and mother died. Lots of men would have walked off and left me." He started running across the sand toward the village.

Not until he was on the way home did Ben realize who Martin reminded him of—Deming Jarves. Although outwardly the two couldn't have been more dissimilar, they shared the same burning enthusiasm. What was there about glass that set men's minds on fire?

The next day, when Ben and Phoebe came home from school, Ma was bending over the oven, drawing forth a chocolate cake, its top a shiny brown.

"Can we have some hot?" asked Ben.

"Why do you think I baked it?" asked Ma. "You'd better leave some for supper, though. And Ben, will you dig some clams this afternoon? I want to make a chowder for supper."

"Can I go, too?" Phoebe asked eagerly.

"There's your sampler to finish," said Ma. "Aunt Lettie is due to arrive any day now."

"Boys have all the fun," said Phoebe. "I don't believe what that old verse says, anyway." She stamped off wrathfully and returned a minute later, holding up her sampler and chanting,

"When youth's soft season shall be o'er,
And scenes of childhood charm no more,
My riper years with joy shall see
This proof of youthful industry."

Thrusting the needlework under her mother's nose, she demanded, "Would you look with joy on such a proof of youthful industry? All I'll think of are my pricked fingers and the fun I missed."

"At least you're learning to sew very nicely," said Ma. "I'm sure Aunt Lettie will be happy to see how you've progressed."

A half hour later, as Ben sauntered over the dunes, he could feel a little sorry for Phoebe. There had never been a more beautiful day. His bare toes felt cool and free against the sand. The breeze ruffled his hair, and when he reached the top of a high dune he felt almost light enough to fly.

Out on the flats he plunged his clam fork at an angle beneath a tiny telltale hole. A thin stream of water shot up, and he dug fast. Ah, there was a gray oval shell. A nice fat clam. Nearby was another, then another, and another. In a short time he had tossed dozens into his basket. As the first ripples of the incoming tide washed over his feet he started inland, water dripping from his load.

An army of sandpipers skittered along the beach, wheeled to the right and to the left, then broke ranks to poke needle bills into the sand. At Ben's approach they came to attention and, at some secret signal, flew up into the air with instant precision, as if on a single wing.

Ben had topped the first dunes and was walking along the rough cart track when off to one side he saw a girl in a pink sunbonnet bent over a beach-plum bush, picking the oval garnet fruit. As she lifted her head his breath quickened. Emily had not moved away, after all. Now he'd have a chance to thank her. But as he stood there he couldn't for the life of him think what to say, except to stammer, "I thought you'd left town."

"Whatever gave you that idea?" she asked.

"I never see you at school."

"That's because I'm going to the Academy."

The Academy was a private boarding school on Water Street. Pupils came there from all over Cape Cod, and from as far away as Barbados and Antigua. Few local students went there because of the high fees.

"Why are you going there?" asked Ben. He almost added, "When you could go to the town school for nothing."

"Because I want to be a teacher, and I can learn more there, like music and foreign languages," said Emily. She looked down at the sand, her lashes long on her cheek. "That's why I helped Papa at the store last summer, to earn money for my tuition."

"You must be glad to get away from the store," said Ben. He'd always thought Emily looked odd in that long store apron.

"The funny thing is, I miss it," said Emily. "I liked waiting on people, the nice ones. Some of the women used to tell me about their homes and children. I loved to listen to their way of talking. Of course, some of the men were rough, like the ones that were after you that day."

"You were certainly brave not to give us away," said Ben. "I wish I could thank you properly." Now that the words were out, he realized that it hadn't been hard after all.

She smiled shyly. "After you had gone, I told Papa. He said to let him know right away if anything like that happened again."

"It probably won't," said Ben. Almost before he knew it, he was telling her about the pressing machine, Deming Jarves's flight across the marsh, their talk aboard the *Orion,* the steamboat, and Ira's decision not to build another machine. "He's afraid that the glass blower's children will starve because of his invention," Ben finished.

"That's silly," said Emily. "The only time they come near starving is when their fathers spend all their money on drink." She picked up her basket of beach plums and set out along the track.

"Let me carry your basket," offered Ben. "That's a heavy load for a girl."

"If you really want to, I'd be pleased," said Emily.

Ben matched his step to hers. She could walk pretty well for a girl, with none of those mincing little steps that Phoebe's friends took. As they passed his house he set his clams in the shade of a bush and continued on with Emily.

In no time at all, it seemed, they reached the Griswolds' house, a narrow frame dwelling on River Street.

After he had put Emily's basket on the porch and said good-by, he decided to go a few steps farther and see if Grandfather's copy of the *Columbian Centinel* had come by stage.

The newspaper had not come, but there were two letters for Mrs. Cyrus Tate. Ben hurried home with them.

Shipwreck

One letter was from Pa. He had arrived in Philadelphia and unloaded the glassware without mishap. After taking on the cargo of sand in New Jersey, he would head homeward. In ten days or so he'd be back in Sandwich. The letter was dated a week ago. The family could look for his arrival soon.

The other letter was from Aunt Lettie Bascomb. Its shakily formed words stated that the writer was feeling peaked and not up to making her accustomed trip this fall. If Margaret cared to travel to Chatham, she'd be more than welcome.

Ma looked up, her concern plain. "I'm going down to see her. At ninety-one, anything can be serious. Ben, could you take two or three days off from school to go with me?"

Could he? Ben gave a shout of assent. At the same time he felt a twinge of anxiety. Aunt Lettie's visits were as much a part of autumn as pumpkin pie and fresh cider. In the middle of September she took the stage from Chatham, bringing with her a small trunk bound in calfskin with the hair still on it. She had pipe-stem arms and legs, and a pinched little face covered with fine wrinkles. Her blue eyes were frosty bright, her voice dry and testy. And her knotted fingers were busy all the day, peeling apples, hooking rugs, or piecing quilts.

Nothing daunted Aunt Lettie. Whatever calamity was reported, she could recall an experience that more than matched it. Spunkiness and hard work were her antidotes for every ill. Widowed many years ago, she had subsisted on the pittance her husband had left, remaining serenely independent. Ben found it hard to imagine her sick.

Ma took two days to get ready. She wanted to leave plenty of food prepared ahead, even though Phoebe was a capable little cook, and Honor nearby. Ben's chief concern was Narcissa.

For two weeks he had helped her up and down in the sling, and for the last few days he had removed the canvas support during the day so that she would be free to move around in her stall.

That evening Ben and Phoebe escorted Narcissa out of the barn. Her first steps were wobbly.

"I know just how you feel, Narcissa," Phoebe said soothingly. "I had to learn to walk all over again, too."

The cow gave an uncertain moo and stood still.

"I guess that's enough for now," said Ben, and led her back to the stall. Before he could get the sling underneath her, Narcissa lowered herself to the floor and lay quietly in the straw.

"She got down all by herself," crowed Phoebe.

Ben folded the old hammock and put it on a shelf. Now he could go off to Chatham with a free mind.

Two mornings later Ma was up before daybreak. At the first clank of stove lids, Ben was out of bed and pulling on clean clothes. The world was still dark when they drove out of the yard. In the back of the buggy was a bag of feed for the horse, Star, a basket of preserves for Aunt Lettie, and a bulging lunch basket.

The wheels rattled along the road. By sunrise they had reached Barnstable. As the morning wore on, Ben saw farmers gathering in the last of their crops and women picking cranberries in the bogs. When the sun was high overhead they stopped for dinner under a broad oak on a hilltop where they could look far away across rolling hills to the blue sea in the distance.

"That's the outside shore," said Ma. "Your father is somewhere out there in the *Orion*. I hope we get home before he does."

Then it was Ben's turn to drive. At the foot of the hill they came to a sandy stretch where the narrow wheels sank almost to the hubs. Soon they were back on gravel, and a short while later they passed with a whisper over layers of pine needles.

It was a long trip. They didn't stop for supper, but munched on ham sandwiches and apples as they rolled along. Soon Ma began to recognize landmarks.

"There's the fork in the road where we turn," she said. "It's just a little way now. I hope Aunt Lettie hasn't gone to bed."

Lights were shining in the windows of the small cottage when they drew up, and smoke fluttered out of the chimney. Star blew noisily through his nostrils as if he knew he had reached his destination. The door opened, and a woman peered out. She was so tall and stout that she filled the doorway.

"Oh, dear," exclaimed Ma. "Something's wrong." She climbed stiffly down.

How wrong they discovered a minute later when they entered the house. In the main room, resting on two sawhorses, stood a coffin, its pine boards pale in the candlelight. The woman, a neighbor, had discovered Aunt Lettie that morning when she had come to return a quilt pattern. She had let herself in by the door, which was never locked, and was astonished to find the stove cold and the bedroom door shut. Aunt Lettie had slipped out quietly in her sleep, as little trouble to anyone in death as in life. In the absence of any family members, the neighbor had arranged with the minister for the burial.

"You're her niece, her only living relative?" asked the woman after Ma had identified herself. "Sent by the Lord, I do believe."

"I wish he'd sent me two days earlier," said Ma. She took a long breath and looked at the woman. "You've been good to make all the arrangements. The burial will be tomorrow at four, you say? I imagine you'd like to go home and rest. Ben and I can look after things here."

"I'm sorry you've such a sad end to your journey," said the woman, "but I'm glad you got here when you did."

When she had left, Ben unloaded the buggy and gave

Star a bag of oats. He put his blanket on him and tied him under a tree. Tying him seemed silly, in a way. Star was probably too tired to take another step.

Ma started a fire and made hot tea. She put fresh sheets on Aunt Lettie's bed and told Ben to sleep there. It was the only bed in the house. She would sit up through the night with Aunt Lettie, as was fitting. Reluctantly Ben obeyed. He thought of offering to sit up with her, but his eyes were already closing.

In the morning he found Ma stretched on the sofa, her face pale and drawn, looking almost lifeless herself.

The weather had changed during the night. In mid-morning a surly wind arose, whining among the scrub pines that surrounded the cottage. It whistled in the chimney while Ma cooked dinner, and the fire roared and flared. By the middle of the afternoon the trees were bending, and on the roof a shingle tore loose, danced across its fellows, and sailed away.

Ben led Star to the neighbor's barn, asked her permission, and tied him inside. The horse pawed the strange floor and neighed nervously. Ben stayed with him for a while, feeling just as uneasy. The neighbor woman came out with a shawl over her head.

"Would your mother mind much if I didn't come to the cemetery? My youngest took sick during the night."

"I'm sure she'd understand," said Ben.

When he got back to the cottage, the minister had arrived. A large, strapping fellow in his twenties, he had a full face and round blue eyes.

"Your aunt made the most of her life, not just the

best of it," he said to Ma. "She was a good example for us all."

Soon a man drove up in an open wagon. He was wearing a long black coat and a black stovepipe hat tied on with a strip of cloth. The wind blew his coat tight against his hollow chest and sagging stomach. With him were three other men, also clad in black, with woolen caps pulled tight over their ears.

"Don't know as we'll have many mourners," he said to Ma. "This looks like a bad storm." He stared disapprovingly at Ma's green dress.

"I didn't come prepared for a funeral," she said shortly.

"If you're ready, ma'am, we'll start out now. I'd like to get this over before the rain comes." The man gestured to his companions. The four lifted the coffin and placed it on the wagon.

When Ma had closed the door, the man said, "Mourners usually walk behind the hearse, but seeing as you're the only lady, perhaps you'd like to ride up here with me."

"No, thank you," said Ma with dignity. "I'll walk with my son and the minister." Under her breath she sputtered, "The very idea!"

The walk to the cemetery was mercifully short. The wind tugged at their clothes, whipping Ma's skirts around her ankles and nearly carrying away her bonnet. Ben was cold, his shirt and jacket like gauze under the chilly blasts.

They climbed a deserted hill, its few houses shuttered against the storm. Behind them stalked the three assistants. At the top of the hill the force of the wind nearly took their breath away. They looked out across a gray, ugly sea covered with the crests of whitecaps. Below, midway between the hilltop and the shore, lay the cemetery, its sparse grass flattened by successive gusts.

At the graveside the undertaker and his assistants lowered the coffin into the waiting space. The minister opened his prayer book. The wind whipped the pages and almost tore the book from his hands. He gripped the volume, and as if defying the storm, started to read.

Ben caught a few words. "In my Father's house are many mansions." He wondered if Aunt Lettie would be happy in a mansion. Her own home was as spare and scoured as a sea shell. "If it were not so, I would have told you." Only now and then could he hear a phrase; most of the words were caught and carried away.

A drop of rain hit Ben's cheek. He turned his head and looked out on the heaving ocean. Tossing on the angry waters was a sight he would have given his right arm not to see. There was no mistaking that familiar hull, those worn sails. It was the *Orion,* and from the sluggish way she was bucking each wave, then sinking back into the trough, he guessed she was in trouble.

Without thinking, Ben touched his mother's arm. She followed his gaze, and gave a gasp, her face turning as white as marble. Going up to the minister, she shouted in his ear, "Will you bring the service to a close quickly? My husband's ship is out there, and I fear he is in danger. My duty to my aunt is done; I must think of the living."

An hour later Ben and his mother stood on a high

dune, straining their eyes to catch a glimpse through rain and salt spray of the *Orion*. Tremendous breakers thundered against the sand, pushing it forward, then back, with an unceasing hiss. The wind was even fiercer than it had been before.

In a lull between gusts Ben saw the *Orion*. About a half a mile away, it lay at an unnatural angle, its bow tilted upward. Waves washed over its afterdeck. The mainmast was down, and he thought he could see men cutting away the rigging. Then the rain curtain closed down, and he could see no more of the ship.

The minister had come to the shore with them, then gone at once for help.

Nearby stood a solitary house, as weathered as the driftwood that littered its yard. The side toward the sea had no windows; it presented a blind, bleached wall. Any other time Ben would have wondered at the lack of openings for light and air. Today he understood. If there had been glass, every pane would be ground by flying sand and frosted with salt—or blown in by the gale.

A woman appeared at the side of the house, pointed to the two on the beach, and to her home.

"I thinks she wants you to go inside," said Ben in Ma's ear.

"Not now," she said tautly. Her eyes were fixed on the spot where she had last seen the schooner, as if by the very intensity of her thought she could keep it safe. Her lips moved, and Ben could tell she was saying his father's name over and over again, like a prayer, "Cyrus, oh, Cyrus."

On the cliff above the beach four men appeared, the minister and three others, hauling a whaleboat on a low cart. They eased it over a crest and down the steep grade. At the water's edge they pulled out oars and laid them across the thwarts.

A short, bulky man with a hooked nose and jutting chin looked out toward the *Orion* and back again, as if measuring the distance.

"Ready, Elijah?" a second man shouted to him.

"We'll need two more," bellowed Elijah. He jerked his thumb at the minister, who tore off his long coat and handed it to Ma. Then he pointed his chin at Ben and yelled, "Can you row?"

Ben leaped to the side of the boat and grasped the gunwale. He helped shove the craft into the surf, wading out hip-deep, and when his turn came, between the breaking of the giant rollers, climbed into the pitching craft. Elijah took up a position at the stern, his powerful arms wrapped around the steering oar.

Ben's first stroke nearly sent him toppling. He had never handled an oar so long or so heavy. There was no time to learn gradually. He had to master the giant oar at once if the whaleboat were not to turn broadside to the breakers and capsize.

As the boat dipped down into a trough he thrust his oar deep into the marbled water. The next moment the sturdy craft rose up, up, up to top a mountain of green. He'd never known there was such savage force. Bracing his heels against the ribs of the boat, he heaved with all his might, trying to match the stroke of the man beside him, and keeping his eyes on the minister's powerful shoulders in front of him.

Ma's lone figure on the beach was soon lost to view. The world was one frothing wave after another. Icy spray struck against his back. His arms ached with the strain; he had a pain under one shoulder blade. Would they never reach the schooner?

A shout from Elijah, and the men slowed their strokes. The *Orion* was just ahead. With infinite caution the steersman maneuvered the whaleboat toward the schooner's leeward side. On the forward deck, clinging to the downed foremast, were Captain Tate, Caleb, and the four crew members, drenched and near exhaustion.

Caleb's tanned face split in a wide smile. He shouted something, but the wind tore his words away. Captain Tate balanced himself on the slanting deck and tossed a line to the whaleboat. Elijah caught it with one powerful hand and made it fast. The space between the two craft lessened as the men hauled on the line.

The *Orion*'s crew worked their way to the rail. At a shout from Elijah, one hurled himself over and landed in the whaleboat. The vessel rocked dangerously. The men at the oars fought to keep it steady. Almost before the first man had crouched on the bottom, a second jumped.

The third man missed by a matter of inches. Elijah roared at the minister, who slid his oar into his seatmate's fist and leaned far over the side. In seconds he had grasped the man's collar, then his shoulders, and heaved him aboard. The fourth crewman made a clean jump, and there were left on the *Orion* just Caleb and the captain.

The whaleboat was heavily loaded, its gunwales periously close to the water. Elijah held aloft one beefy hand, with a single finger pointing upward.

Ben would never forget the next minutes. Caleb held back, gesturing to Captain Tate to follow the crew. The captain stood firm as a rock. Ben could see that his jaw was set, as he had seen it a thousand times before.

Ben thought of Ma on the shore, waiting for Pa. He heard her cry, Cyrus, oh, Cyrus. Pa was important to her, to the whole family. As for Ben himself, he was of no special account. He'd give Pa his place.

He had taken one hand from the oar and was struggling to rise when he heard a thundering, "Stay on that oar!" from Elijah. The prophet himself couldn't have voiced more awesome authority. Ben sank back in his place, renewed his grip, and cast an anguished glance toward the two men on the *Orion*.

Elijah roared again, a wordless bellow. Ben knew he meant that he couldn't hold the whaleboat in this position much longer.

Caleb must have realized the futility of his attempt. His face tragic, he gathered himself together and leaped. Almost before he struck he had found the place where he would best balance the craft and huddled down, his head between his knees.

Elijah swung the whaleboat around toward shore. The men bent to their oars, and Ben shouted, "We'll come back for you, Pa!"

Then he was pulling for all he was worth, hating

every stroke that carried him away from his father, and sick with disgust that after such great effort there had not been room enough for the one most important to him. For a short time he could see his father standing alone on the *Orion;* then mountainous seas hid him from view.

Ben had thought that the trip out to the schooner was an almost overwhelming struggle. On the way back to shore he realized that the rescuers were working against even more powerful odds. The weight of the five ship-wrecked men made the boat twice as hard to row. Now and then a wave threw gallons of water into the craft. The crouching men bailed frantically.

Dip, pull, lift; dip, pull, lift. Ben might have given up if it hadn't been for the minister's steady pull. There was a quiet strength about the young man that gave Ben heart. If he can do it, so can I, Ben told himself. He kept to the grueling task.

Beneath the whistle of the wind thudded the crash of breakers. A few strokes more, and the whaleboat's keel grated on the sand. In desperate urgency the men tumbled over the side, and as the next wave threatened to cover them, drew the whaleboat up on the beach.

Reeling from fatigue, Ben stared about. The air was gray with twilight. Some hundred yards away was the solitary house. And hurrying toward him, her long skirts twisting, was Ma. He staggered toward her, wondering how he would tell her. He never had to. Her wild glance raced over the figures of the men, once, twice, and then came to rest on Ben.

"We're going back to get him, Ma," he cried in

robust denial of any possibility that the *Orion* might have already sunk.

She gave him one tragic look and lifted her eyes to the sky. He saw then how swiftly it had darkened. Only with difficulty could he identify the other figures on the beach.

Elijah spoke in a voice of doom. "It's too late to go out again. We'd never be able to find the vessel at night."

In the wind-swept house above the dunes there was hot food and fire, but no comfort for the heartsick. During the long night Ma said not a word. Silently she listened to Caleb's jerky sentences.

"It wasn't the captain's fault; he knows the shore well. He'd not sailed with a hold full of sand before. It's different from lumber, heavy and apt to shift. Bad seas opened the forward seams. The sand got wet and was heavier than ever. With the wind and tide forcing us inshore, and the vessel so logy, we hadn't a chance." He groaned. "I should have made him leave the ship instead of me."

Wound up in a blanket on the floor, Ben dozed in fits and starts. At first light he got creakily to his feet and found Ma already outside, peering distractedly through the grayness.

Together they watched the eastern sky lighten and a brightness come into the world. But the black of night was still in their hearts, for where yesterday the *Orion* had tossed, there was today an unbroken expanse of water.

The Stranger

Late one November afternoon two months later Ben slapped the reins along the horses' backs and urged them down the road toward Fessenden's inn. The wagon was heaped high with kindling Ben had split that day. If he hurried, he could stack it in the tavern shed before suppertime.

The air was cold and raw, blowing in from the sea with a penetrating dampness. Ben hunched his shoulders, weary from the hard work of that day, and the day before, and the day before that.

From the day the *Orion* had sunk, things had gone badly with the Tate family. The loss of Pa had stunned them all. Ben wondered if Ma would ever recover from the shock. Not that she talked about it. On the contrary, she had mentioned it but once. After the day-long vigil on the beach, watching for the body that was never washed up, she had said only, "This is what I've feared since the day Cyrus and I were promised. Knowing that it might happen doesn't make it a mite easier to bear now that it has come."

Grandfather had collapsed at news of the disaster and lain helpless for days. Although he regained some strength, he seemed to have lost all interest in life and become an aged, querulous, feeble old man. His hatred of the glass factory was an overwhelming obsession, toward which he directed the remnant of his burned-out energy.

As if the loss of Pa were not enough, the family was now threatened with the loss of the house. Taxes were taxes, and though Tates had lived in Sandwich for generations, the sudden death of the family's head was no excuse for not paying their share of town expenses.

Ben had never thought much about money. There had always been enough to eat and to wear, and fire to keep them warm. Now the need for hard cash drove him during the days and haunted him at night. One evening after Phoebe had gone to bed, Ma had spoken to Grandfather.

"Father Tate, do you have money enough to pay our taxes?"

The old man had harrumphed gloomily. "I handed over every penny to Cyrus to get stores for the *Orion* his last trip." He lifted the newspaper in front of his face. Ben knew how he hated to let anyone see the tears that came so frequently to his eyes nowadays.

"If it weren't for that blackguard Jarves, Cyrus would be alive today," he said from behind the paper. "It's all his fault, damn him."

There was a long silence, and then Ma said, "I had hoped there would be something coming to me from the sale of Aunt Lettie's house, but the mortgage holder took it all, and rightly so. Though I've tried to be careful with what Cyrus gave me, there's very little left. If it weren't for Ben selling wood, I don't know how we'd manage."

The next day Ben had quit school, and now he spent all his time cutting and hauling wood. Ma had protested, but she accepted thankfully the coins he gave her. The trees that were mature enough to cut were coming down, one by one. Soon there would be no more wood to sell. A wood lot that was sufficient for one family could not be expected to furnish money enough for its entire support.

As the wagon creakily approached Fessenden's, Ben heard voices and laughter coming from the brightly lighted windows and doorway. Carriages and riding horses filled the rear innyard. He had a hard time maneuvering his wagon near the shed.

As he filled his arms with split pieces the kitchen door opened, letting forth the rich aroma of roasting beef. Ben's nostrils quivered, and his mouth watered. He hadn't had roast beef since that night in Boston with Mr. Jarves and his father and Caleb.

Inside the kitchen, waiters were rushing around, and the cook was shouting. One of his helpers ran out the back door with a bucket of potato peelings and shouted to Ben, "Daniel Webster's here tonight, and a lot of bigwigs from Boston. And are we busy!"

Ben laid the kindling in a neat row against the shed wall. One armful after another he piled up, until the wagon was empty and the stack in the shed shoulder high. He brushed off his hands and went to the kitchen door.

The tantalizing fragrance of rich foods was almost more than he could bear. He had to speak twice to the cook before he could get his attention. Mustaches quivering in his red face, the man said, "You'll have to see Mr. Fessenden, and he's busy now. Say, how would you like to earn some extra money? I can't spare anybody to wash dishes, and we're running out of plates."

Ben rolled up his sleeves. He had never seen such a hubbub, with folks dashing here and there, and everyone talking at once. He found a kettle of boiling water on the stove, poured some of it into a wooden tub, scooped soft soap out of a smaller tub, added cold water from the pump, and went to work.

Two hours later he had cleared away what had been a mountain of greasy cutlery and dishes. The rush was over. He dried his hands, rolled down his sleeves, and went to the cook again.

The rotund man, carving knife in hand, was cutting pale-pink slices of beef from a gigantic roast. Ben was nearly drooling.

"That looks good," he couldn't help saying, wishing he could help himself to a bit.

"How would you like to take a dinner in pay?"

Ben swallowed. There was nothing in the world he'd like better. He could almost taste the succulent meat, feel its juices on his tongue. He had reached for a plate when Ma's face flashed into his mind, her eyes with the deep sad look they had nowadays.

"I'd rather have the money," he said shortly.

The cook looked up in amazement. "You don't know what you're missing," he said. "This is our special banquet."

"The money," said Ben. He didn't trust himself to stay near the roast any longer. In another minute he'd be snatching a piece.

Just then Mr. Fessenden came into the kitchen. The cook spoke to him, and he reached into his pocket. In addition to the dollar for the wood, he added a quarter for the dishwashing.

Ben shot out the door, climbed up on the wagon, and started toward home. His stomach was a hard knot, and the coins in his pocket cold comfort.

At home, Ma pulled a crock of beans from the oven. "I found a nice piece of lean pork in the barrel, just the way you like it."

Beans! When he could have had roast beef. Ben turned his face away so that she couldn't see his scowl. He set the money on the table with a thump.

"Why, Son, there's twenty-five cents more than usual."

"I washed dishes two hours for it," he said shortly.

"A boy washing dishes?" said Phoebe, setting her schoolbooks on the table. She flounced into a chair, and gave a high giggle.

Ben glared at her. "What's so funny about that?" he growled, and attacked the beans, the memory of the roast beef still in his mind.

A light step sounded on the porch, and Honor came in carrying a basket, her cheeks red from the cold. She went to her mother and kissed her. More and more often she came alone to her old home. Caleb seemed to shrink from contact with any of them, most of all with Ma. He had a job driving one of the big bull wagons that carried lumber to the glass factory. Ben had seen him managing the ill-assorted team of a lead horse and two pair of oxen. No one in the family mentioned the fact that a Tate relative was in the employ of the factory.

Honor said brightly, "I tried out that recipe Mrs. Bartlett gave me, the one for sweet rolls. They're quite nice, so I brought some along. Want to try one now, Ben?"

"Mmmm. Still warm." Honor was a nice sister. Ben wished Phoebe were more like her.

"Oh, Mamma," said Phoebe, "you know the poem I'm going to say with Abba Stetson and the other girls? We think it would be proper if we all dressed alike in white dresses. White for purity, you see, since it's a purification party."

"Purification party?" asked Ben. "What's that all about?"

Honor laughed. "Haven't you heard how excited the Cold Water Army got because there was wine punch served at the concert last week? The Army members claim that Academy Hall will never be the same again, and not fit for young folks to step into until it has been purified."

"No, I hadn't heard. I don't have time to sit around and gossip," said Ben sourly.

"I thought Ma might have said something about it," said Honor, then clamped her lips shut, as if remembering that her mother had scarcely been out of the house since Pa had gone.

"Don't you think it's a nice idea for us to dress in white?" pursued Phoebe.

"Wouldn't your Sunday dress do?" asked Ma. "It's a very *light* blue."

"No, Mamma, it has to be white." Phoebe looked soulfully at the ceiling.

"I don't see how we can afford a new white dress," said Ma.

"There's that white stuff with the embroidery in the big chest," offered Phoebe.

"You mean the muslin your father brought me from Cuba?"

"I don't know where it came from, but it's pretty. I'd have the most beautiful dress of all the girls."

Ben glared at his mother. If she gave in to Phoebe—. He remembered the pride with which his father had given the package to Ma. She had unfolded the white lengths reverently, and said, "Oh, Cyrus, it's much too fine."

"Not by a long shot," he had said. "I want you to make it up and wear it when I get back from my next trip."

Other things had intervened, and then had come the fateful last voyage.

As if from a distance, Ben heard his mother say, "Well, if it would make you happy, Phoebe, I suppose you can have it."

"Oh, Mamma!" Phoebe embraced her fervently.

Then she stepped back and said hesitantly, "All the other girls are going to wear white shoes."

"White shoes?" exploded Honor. "I never had a pair of white shoes in my whole life."

"You never had a friend like Abba Stetson, either, an own cousin to the Jarves children," stormed Phoebe.

"I guess I never did," admitted Honor, adding in a low voice that only Ben could hear, "Not that I missed much."

"There's a lovely pair that just fits me at Mr. Murdock's, and he said he'd save them for me," said Phoebe.

"You didn't go in and try them on without asking me?" inquired Ma.

Phoebe lowered her lashes and ducked her chin. "Mrs. Stetson was taking Abba to buy hers, and they invited me to go along. I thought you were so busy it would save you going with me."

"I see," said Ma. Her face was flushed. "Well . . ."

Ben clenched his fist under the table. Shoes cost all of three dollars, as much as would take him four days of hard work to earn. If he had gone without a good roast beef dinner to satisfy the whim of a spoiled little brat! He was ready to explode.

Ma cleared her throat. "I'm sorry, Phoebe, but this time I shall have to disappoint you. We cannot afford white shoes."

"Oh, Mamma," wailed Phoebe. "I'll be a laughing stock. And how can I tell Mr. Murdock that I won't take them?"

"I'll go with you tomorrow after school," offered

Honor. "We must let him know right away in case he has a chance to sell them to someone else."

"Somebody else wearing my white shoes!" Phoebe sobbed, and ran from the room.

In the days following, there were regular announcements by Phoebe on the development of plans for the purification party. It would be held at night. There would be recitations and singing to the accompaniment of a string quartet. The climax of the evening would be the girls' program. Phoebe would not tell what it was, but said that Mr. Stetson had furnished a dozen little glass pails for the occasion.

Sometimes Ben heard her repeating snatches of verse. At his approach she would close her lips tightly and take on a mysterious look. One day she disclosed that a new girl had been invited to join the group. She learned so fast that she knew the words and music of the song even better than some of those who had been practicing every afternoon. She didn't stay afterward to talk but hurried home to help her aunt, who kept house for her father. Her name was Emily.

Ben had thought wild horses couldn't drag him to the purification party. Now he decided he might as well look in for a few minutes. Ma would probably make him take Phoebe anyway.

There was so much talk about clothes that Ben wondered about his own tight suit. He thought of Pa's Sunday clothes hanging under a dust cover in the closet. He got up the courage to ask Ma if he might wear them, but the look on her face was too much. He'd never mention them again. He couldn't help being jealous. Ma was cutting up the embroidered muslin for Phoebe, but she wouldn't even let him borrow Pa's suit. It wasn't fair!

At noontime on the day of the party, Ira stepped out of his doorway and waved. Ben, on his way home from delivering wood, pulled the horses to a halt.

"I was down to Mr. Murdock's for some new boots this morning," said Ira. "He needs someone to help him tend store. I thought thee might ask for the job. Thy wood lot is cut nigh to the limit."

"I'll go down this afternoon," said Ben. "Thank you, Ira." No need to comment on the wood lot. He knew as well as Ira that there weren't more than two cords of timber left.

After dinner he doused his face in a basin of water, scrubbed behind his ears, and wet his thick thatch and combed it. The face in the small looking glass over the sink looked older. He hoped Mr. Murdock would think he appeared responsible enough to help in the store.

A short while later Ben mounted the two broad steps to the shoe store and opened the door. The bell jangled, and Mr. Murdock looked down from a ladder on which he was perched, stacking boxes on the top shelf.

"Do you want to buy something?" he asked testily, "or do you just want to look at shoes, like your sister?"

Ben flushed. It wasn't his fault that Phoebe hadn't been able to buy the white shoes.

"I heard you were looking for someone to tend store," he said.

"Not any more, I ain't," said Mr. Murdock. "Hired somebody else no more than ten minutes ago. He's out back sweeping, now."

Ben left quickly, the bell jangling maliciously behind him.

Just down the road, the stage drew up in front of the inn, the horses lathered and blowing noisily. The driver stepped down from his high seat and marched into the tavern with the leather sack of mail, leaving the passengers to descend as best they might.

No ladies aboard this trip, thought Ben. When there were, the driver was a regular gallant, bowing and scraping for all he was worth.

The coach door opened, and Ben couldn't help staring at the man who emerged. He wore a broad-brimmed black hat unlike the tall beavers of most travelers, and a fringe of tight black curls touched the collar of his dark green cape. As he stepped down from the coach, carrying a small satchel, his foot caught, and he fell in an awkward sprawl. Ben sprang forward and helped him to his feet. The satchel had burst open and its contents spilled upon the ground—some tools that had been wrapped in a piece of cloth woven in a bright design. Ben recognized the tongs, compass, and shears used by glassmakers. He knelt down to pick them up, and almost bumped heads with the man. For a moment their eyes met. In a flash Ben felt that he would like to know him better. The stranger's face was lined and worn, but his mouth had strength and firmess, and his eyes a deep wisdom.

They stood up, the man coming barely to Ben's shoulder.

"*Danke schön.*" The newcomer extended a scarred hand.

Ben didn't need to understand the words to recognize the man's gratitude. "You're welcome," he said, and returned the firm handclasp.

The man turned his head this way and that, as if seeking some particular place. *"Wo ist die Glasfabrik?"* he said.

Whatever language the man was speaking, it was near enough to English for Ben to comprehend. "Down there," he said, pointing to the tall chimneyed building.

"Oh, ja," said the man. *"Herr Jarves? Dies ist die Glasfabrik von Herrn Jarves?"*

For a minute Ben hesitated. Mr. Jarves was away, but he was still the head of the factory.

"Yes, that's Mr. Jarves's factory," he said.

The stranger smiled. *"Danke,"* he said, and turned down Dock Lane. He walked slowly, as if he were very tired or very weak.

Ben headed homeward. He might as well get busy on what was left of the standing timber. At least he'd get a little more money out of the wood lot.

The stranger's question about Mr. Jarves had brought back thoughts of the pressing machine. If only Ira had not refused to build another. Ben could envision the machine as it had been on that summer day, the wooden mold smoking and hissing. The molds should be made of metal, so they wouldn't char. And there could be a whole row of molds, each with its own plunger, all operated by the same main lever. He wanted badly to talk about his idea with someone. Ira was so dead set against the machine he probably wouldn't listen. Ben wished Mr. Jarves would return to Sandwich so that they could talk. But even as he wished, he realized how futile the thought was. After all that had happened, he couldn't approach Mr. Jarves. Someone would be sure to see him and tell Grandfather, and then there would be trouble.

The Purification Party

Just before supper Ben found Phoebe in the barn in her stocking feet. She had a pail of a thin white mixture, which she was daubing on her brown shoes.

"What do you think you're doing?" he asked.

Phoebe's face turned crimson. "Don't laugh at me, Ben. I couldn't bear to be the only one different. I'm whitewashing my shoes."

"It's no laughing matter," he said scornfully. "You'll ruin your shoes. The lime in the whitewash will take all the oil out of the leather."

"I don't care," said Phoebe defiantly. "I've got to be like the others."

At the last minute, when they were ready to set out for the purification party, Ma decided she would stay home. "I keep thinking, suppose by some miracle your father wasn't drowned and he came home. I'd never forgive myself if I weren't here to welcome him."

Ben couldn't bear to look at her. How could she cherish such a hope when she knew as well as he that the *Orion* had gone down?

Phoebe and Ben rode in the buggy to the Academy and tied Star in one of the stalls in the open shed. Phoebe dashed off to join the other girls in giggling nervousness until the time for their part in the program. Ben looked about for a seat. There was one in the back of the hall beside a dark-haired girl. Why wasn't Emily with the other members of the purification chorus? He tried not to feel self-conscious as he made his way toward her.

"Hello, Ben," Emily said cheerily. "How nice that you could come."

"I thought you were going to be in the girls' program," he said.

"I was, but I didn't have a white dress." She smoothed the skirt of her dark-red merino.

"I'm glad you didn't," Ben blurted, then added, "I mean that if you had one, you wouldn't be here in the audience. Will it be all right if I sit with you?"

The program opened with a declamation by Mrs. Eugene Tarbox on the evils of drink. She painted a horrible picture of the demon alcohol's dreadful effects on family life. Then came a solo by Mr. Cassius Abercrombie. His bass voice shook the windows with its resonance. He was followed by the string quartet, and then by Miss Amy Blossom, who gave a recitation with appropriate gestures on the early death of one of liquor's tragic victims.

There was a hush, whispers from behind curtains at the end of the hall, and in marched twelve young girls, two by two. At the head were Abba Stetson and Phoebe.

All wore white dresses. Phoebe's was by far the prettiest, though the very sight of it made Ben resentful.

Each girl carried a small glass pail filled with water. They ranged themselves in a line in front of the audience, and sang:

> With purifying water
> We come to Academy Hall
> Our hearts are filled with sadness
> As we listen to the call.

The young faces took on mournful expressions, and the girls continued:

> We sorrow that the wine cup
> Has passed at Academy Hall
> And we sorrow for our young men
> Lest with its snare they fall.

With anxious glances to be sure they were acting in unison, the singers raised their pails on high.

> Fresh water from the fountain
> We've brought to Academy Hall—

One by one the young voices trailed off uncertainly. Worried faces turned white, then pink. In the awkward silence clear tones rose from beside Ben:

> An emblem of the purity
> That should reign at Academy Hall.

Emily could sing better than any of the other girls, Ben realized.

The chorus finished the verse with more enthusiasm than harmony, formed a single line, and walked up and down the aisles, scattering drops of water from the pails and chanting with great spirit, as if to make up for their former lapse:

Cold water, pure water,
Cold water for me,
And *ruin* for the trembling
De-bau-chee!

The last word was shouted with great indignation.

As Phoebe drew near, Ben noticed that she was sprinkling with such vigor that water had spilled on her shoes. Rivulets ran down the whitewashed surface, leaving streaks of brown. The girl behind her stopped scattering purifying drops long enough to point to Phoebe's feet, and gave a muffled laugh. Phoebe looked down and a slow flush rose over her face, but she did not miss a word. "And *ruin* for the trembling debauchee!" she sang very loudly.

When the program was over, there were refreshments —cocoa for the young people, and tea for their elders. Ben overheard that punch had been proposed and tabooed—a spy from the opposition might sneak in and add certain forbidden ingredients! It was easy to sense the relief of those in charge as the evening drew to a close. There had been rumors that slaves of the demon alcohol might introduce some unexpected and unwelcome excitement into the party.

When the last crumb of cake had been eaten and the last cooky devoured, people began to leave. Ben, with Emily and Phoebe, was at the top of the stairs when he heard Mr. Murdock, at the bottom, let out a roar of rage. As the crowd went outside there were more cries and bellows of protest.

The horses that two hours before had been left properly harnessed had during the program been removed from their traces and put back between the shafts— backward. Where one expected to see a horse's head, there was a broad rump and switching tail. Where one expected to see the hindquarters, there was a beast with a puzzled face and inquiring eyes, nibbling at the dashboard.

Emily began to chuckle. "Did you ever see anything so funny? Look at Deacon Bassett's mare. She seems really offended!"

Ben could almost hear the mare saying, Who would dare to do this undignified thing to *me?*

For a few minutes all was bedlam. Some of the men ran into the shadows and down the street, looking for the culprits. Cries of "What an outrage!" and "This is monstrous!" filled the air. Soon there was another shout. "It's those drunkards from the factory village. They did this!"

Ben was laughing too hard to join the hunt. Besides, he didn't see why anyone should be seriously angry, and secretly wished that he had thought of such a prank.

While Ben was buckling the last of the harness Emily patted Star. "It must be nice to own a horse," she said.

"Don't you have one?" asked Phoebe, her tone implying that everybody had a horse.

"We don't really need one," said Emily, stroking Star's mane. "My, but you're a real pet," she said as he turned his head toward her.

"Star's like one of the family," said Ben. "How would you like to drive him home, Emily?"

"Could I? I've never driven a horse in my life."

"Nothing to it," said Ben. He helped her up, then Phoebe, and climbed in on the opposite side, so that Emily was in the middle. He handed her the reins. "Give them a little slap," he directed, "then pull on the left so he'll turn into Water Street."

Emily was sitting up very straight. She held the reins with a firm yet light touch, and she looked happy enough to burst. He wished she lived five miles out of town so the ride could be longer.

"My father was worried about my coming home alone. He has a bad cold and had to stay indoors. And Aunt Cassie hates to walk even a little way, so I went by myself tonight. Wait till I tell them that I drove a real horse!"

The night was clear and frosty, the stars very bright. Somewhere in the distance a wolf howled. Star's hoofs clip-clopped over the frozen ground.

Emily's house was the smallest on River Street. Near a lamp in the window sat a man wrapped to the chin in a dressing gown.

"There's Papa now," said Emily. "Thank you for letting me drive." She jumped down and gave Star a goodnight pat.

When Star came to the crossroads, Ben saw two men coming down the main highway from the direction of Boston. He looked at them curiously but could not make out their faces in the starlight. Only the Bassetts lived down that way. They had been at the meeting and were doubtless home by now. Why were these two traveling the opposite way from the rest of the townsfolk?

Phoebe was silent the rest of the way, and when Ben came in from unharnessing Star, he found her at the kitchen sink, sadly examining her shoes.

"I've got to get this white stuff off," she said. "Do you really think my shoes are ruined?"

Ben couldn't say a word. The shoes were certainly a mess. The whitewash had dried to a paste that cracked with each step, and the drops of purifying water had dissolved the white covering, exposing ugly brown patches.

Phoebe took up a brush, wet it, and began to scrub. "I'm so tired of being poor," she lamented. "I wish I could have pretty things like the other girls, and go on trips to Boston, and have more than just one old pair of shoes!" She burst into tears.

"I know how you feel," said Ben. "I'd like another suit, and something to eat besides fish and clams— something like roast beef."

Phoebe stopped her wailing. "Why, Ben, I didn't know you felt that way. Of course you need a new suit. The way your arms and legs stick out of that old one is positively—positively *ludicrous*."

Ben inspected his wrists and ankles. So he looked ludicrous, did he? For a few minutes he fumed inwardly while Phoebe scrubbed away, fresh tears falling on her shoes.

"Salt water's the worst thing for leather," he said. "I'll get some oil from the shed and put that on. Your shoes ought to look better in the morning. In fact, everything will."

A more cheerful Phoebe went up to bed, yawning sleepily. Ben followed her upstairs, but not to bed. He had never been more wide awake in his life.

What the Tate family needed was money. But where could he earn it? Any other person in Sandwich could go to the glass factory for work, but there was no point in his even considering the possibility, with Grandfather so set against the glassworks. He had been disturbed enough that his son had carried shipments for Mr. Jarves. If his grandson were to be employed in that detested factory, he might fall into a fatal rage.

There was also the hostility of the glassworkers. If Ben should seek employment at the works, they might recognize him as one of those who had jeopardized their livelihood. He remembered their raised fists and shouted threats when he and Ira had fled. He had no desire to encounter their enmity again.

In the winter there was practically no other work available in Sandwich. No one looked for extra hands for haying, reaping, and harvesting as they did in summer. He might get a few days' work cutting ice, but that was limited. No, he must look elsewhere.

Into his mind flashed a memory of the steamboat, and the captain, saying, "Any time you're looking for a job, come and see me."

Boston. That was where he would go. He felt wildly elated at the prospect. It had been so exciting to work around the steam engine that he would be willing to do it for nothing if he didn't have to send money home. Probably the job paid well; he'd heard about the big pay people got in cities.

He looked out the window at the starlit night. Why not start right away? He was too excited to sleep, and if he went now he could leave a note for Ma. Then he wouldn't have to argue with her.

Half an hour later he was ready. He weighed the possibility of taking a few coins from the carved wooden box Ma used as a bank. But no, she would need every penny. When he got hungry he'd chop wood or wash dishes for a meal.

He let himself out the back door and closed it softly. He tiptoed past the barn lest Star whicker or Narcissa low, then walked across grass crisp with frost to the road. The night was cold, for a fact! His breath came out in a cloud.

In front of Ira's he said a silent good-by. His skiff was pulled up on the bank of the creek where he had left it a week ago. He stopped long enough to turn it over so snow and ice wouldn't settle in it. He wished he had time to draw it up by the barn. Maybe Ira would take care of it when he knew Ben was far away.

Branches creaked overhead. Somewhere a dog barked, and on the ridge a wolf howled. Ben's footsteps seemed very loud on the frozen surface of the road. When he reached the crossroads, he turned to the right, down the main highway to Boston. How long would it take to walk that far? The stage took a day. Could he, with his long legs, cover it in two or three? He lengthened his stride.

Just beyond the Bassett house he heard a faint cry from the ditch. He looked in the direction from which it had come, but saw only shadows. Probably one of the

Bassetts' cats—they had three, all death on birds and squirrels. He walked on. The cry came again, louder and unmistakably human.

In seconds Ben had found its source, and knelt beside a barely conscious figure at the side of the road. In the darkness he could tell only that it was a man. As he leaned close he heard a hoarse *"Hilfe."*

There was no doubt as to the man's identity. This was the stranger who had asked the way to the glass factory.

Ben put one arm under his shoulders and raised his head. The man was shaking with cold. His teeth were chattering. If he were left here, he'd freeze to death before morning. Ben's fingers encountered something wet and sticky. It was blood, trickling from a wound in the man's head. Suddenly, from nearby, came the howl of wolves. They might smell the blood, and then the man would have more to fear than cold.

"Shall I take you to the inn?" Ben asked, raising the man to a sitting position. As he spoke he realized how futile the question was. If the man had a room at the inn, he'd be in it now, sound asleep. And if he had any friends, he would be with them, not here on the highway, half dead with cold and a gash on the head.

They could not remain here any longer, that was certain. Again came the wolf cry, its menace real and close. Ben heaved the stranger to his feet and half carried him a few paces. The man's feet dragged. They couldn't go very far at this rate. Ben lowered the man to the base of a tree, letting him rest against it, then started away, intending to go for Star and the buggy.

The man clung to him frantically, crying, *"Nein,*

nein." He was so terrified that Ben again helped him to his feet and along the road. The Bassett house was nearby. He'd waken Deacon Bassett and see if he would take the man in.

Half carrying the injured man, Ben made his way to the front door and hammered on it with his fist, until a light appeared in an upstairs window. Minutes later the door creaked open.

"What's the trouble? Have the British landed again?" The deacon's nightcap was askew. He had fought in 1812 and had no faith in treaties. He peered past his candle at the two on his doorstep. "Young Tate, what are you doing out at this hour? And who's that with you?"

"I found him just up the road. He's hurt and needs help."

The deacon held the candle near the slumping figure. "I can't be expected to take in every drunken foreigner that falls down in front of my house." He started to close the door.

"What shall I do with him?" asked Ben.

"That's your lookout," said the deacon, "and you'd better be more careful of the company you keep." He slammed the door. Ben could hear the bolt sliding shut, and lost his temper.

Putting his mouth close to the panels, he shouted, "Didn't you ever hear of the Good Samaritan?"

Anger gave him the strength he needed. Ben hoisted the injured man on his back, struggled down the path, out to the road, and toward home. With every step his half-conscious burden grew heavier. With each minute his own breath grew shorter, and his legs weaker. After what seemed hours he reached home, freed one hand to lift the latch, and stumbled into the kitchen, lowering the man to the floor.

The first thing was to get him warm. Ben lighted the lamp and looked in the stove. Ah, there was still a red glow in the firebox. He opened the drafts, added kindling and the note he had written to his mother. He was putting the kettle on when Ma came into the room, wearing a dressing gown, her hair in a long braid down her back.

Ben had never been more glad to see her or more grateful for her response to the need of any hurt creature. With a quick intake of breath she bent over the man on the floor and held the lamp near his head.

"He must have fallen and cut his head," Ben said.

Ma said sharply, "He didn't get *that* wound from a fall. Somebody struck him."

Swiftly she made up a bed in the back bedroom just off the kitchen and with Ben's help lifted the man upon it. He seemed barely conscious as she bathed and bound up his head. Together she and Ben eased him out of his clothing and into one of Grandfather's nightshirts, and covered him with quilts. His head fell back upon the pillow, he gave a deep sigh, and went limp.

"Poor thing, he's about done for," murmured Ma. "I wonder if he'll rouse enough to eat some gruel. I'd like to get something into his stomach before he goes sound asleep."

When the thin mixture of oatmeal and milk was ready she spooned some of it into the man's mouth. He managed to swallow a good cupful, then lapsed into slumber.

Ma took the bowl to the sink and pumped water into it. Then she turned to Ben. "Now, Son," she said, "I'd be grateful for some explanation."

The Glassworks

Aching and stiff, with a sour taste in his mouth, Ben woke the next day to a knowledge of disaster. For a moment he lay in the borderland between sleep and consciousness, knowing only that something was wrong, very wrong. Then he remembered. He should have been a third of the way to Boston by now. Instead, he was at home.

Gone was his plan to work on the steamboat; gone his chance to earn enough money to pay the taxes. Instead of making things better, he had made them worse. Now there was another person to be fed and cared for. Last night when he had told Ma why he was on the highway after midnight, he had jettisoned his plan to go to Boston. He could not bear to face again the stricken look that had come into her eyes.

All other ways were barred; only one course was open to him. His duty was as clear as if it were printed in bold, black letters across the wall of his room. He must go to the glass factory and get work. There was simply no other employment in Sandwich. Yet he shrank from the very idea of returning to the glassworks. Under the warm patchwork quilt he could feel cold sweat breaking out on his back.

The bedroom door opened and Phoebe came in. "Don't you know enough to knock?" he growled.

"I thought it was all right. I couldn't hear you getting dressed," Phoebe said, and added, "Mamma wants you to come downstairs. That man is tossing around something fearful. Mamma thinks maybe you can quiet him." Her blue eyes grew round. "Do you think he's bewitched?"

"He's an ogre who eats girls who ask too many questions," snorted Ben. It was some pleasure on such a bleak day to torment Phoebe. "Now scat!"

At the sight of Ben the sick man's eyes softened and he murmured, *"Gut. Gut."* On Ben's shirt sleeve he laid a veined hand. The back was crisscrossed with scars, and the palm bore old callouses. He pointed to himself and said in a hoarse voice, "Karl Gantz."

Ben gave his own name slowly, and added, "I hope you feel better today, Mr. Gantz." Even as he spoke he wondered. The skin stretched across the cheekbones was fiery red, and the eyes seemed too bright.

An hour later Ben was walking down Dock Lane, his feet ringing on the frozen ground, his steps slowing as he drew near the factory. The frosty air was sharp in his nostrils. He had stopped on the way to talk with Caleb. Was there a chance of his driving a bull wagon? Not the slightest, Caleb had said. That was the first work Sandwich farmers thought of. He'd better go to the office.

The streets were deserted at this hour, a little after

eight. Workmen were busy at their tasks indoors; women were getting their children ready for school. At the factory store Ben glanced in the window, wishing he might see a slight, dark-haired girl in a long white apron, although he knew perfectly well Emily was probably getting ready for her classes in the Academy.

Ben quickened his pace. He might as well get it over. Just ahead was the smoky bulk of the glass factory and its sprawl of buildings, and there was the door marked *Office*. He knocked, and at a call from within, turned the knob and entered.

The small room was divided by a wooden railing, behind which, at a desk covered with papers, sat a thin, sour-faced man, writing busily. Ben shut the door and walked toward the desk, his heavy boots making a loud *clump, clump*.

The man lifted his head, squinted over brass-rimmed glasses, and asked, "Looking for work?"

"Yes, sir."

"Experience?" The man spat out the word, extending his lower lip.

"None." The last thing he would mention was the pressing machine, although that had provided experience of a sort.

"You can handle a shovel?"

"Yes, sir."

"Go over to the mixing room. Dan Frisbee needs another man."

"Thank you, sir." Ben turned toward the door.

"Wait a minute," called out the man. "What's your name?" When he had written it down, he squinted at

Ben. "Don't you care what pay you get? Or how many hours you work?"

Ben flushed. Of course he cared.

"Five dollars a week, and you'll work two shifts, each starting at seven. Any questions?"

"Where's the mixing room?"

The man threw back his head and hooted. "You are a greenhorn. The mixing room's between the sand room and the glasshouse. You can go around back, or you can go through the glasshouse."

The glasshouse was the last place Ben wanted to go. He circled around the building. Here at the back, beside the creek, scows were tied up at the factory wharf. Workmen wheeled barrows of sand down ramps from the scows into the open doors of a large room where other men were sifting great mounds of sand.

Farther along was a heavy door. It must lead to the mixing room. Ben tried the knob. The door was locked. He rapped. There was a muffled shout, and a few minutes later Ben could hear a bolt being pushed back and a key turning. The door opened, revealing a man with a broad torso and a square serious face. This must be Dan Frisbee.

"What do you want?" he asked, standing solidly in the opening.

"The man in the office sent me here."

"Are you from a glassmaking family?" Frisbee asked, not budging an inch.

"No." Must he have a relative in the factory to get work here?

"Do you know anybody in the glass business?"

"Not very well. Only Martin O'Connor. He was in my class at school."

"Can you keep your mouth shut?" the man asked, his gray eyes fixed firmly on Ben's.

"Yes, sir."

"You'll do, I guess." He stood aside and beckoned Ben to enter, then shot the bolt and locked the door.

Ben stepped into a room nearly filled with large bins, each containing a different-colored powdery material— red, white, silver, and black. In the center of the room stood a large trough nearly filled with mounds of granules of many hues. A short man with reddish hair was listlessly stirring the mass with a long-handled shovel.

As Ben entered, the man stopped his work, leaned on the shovel, and stared. Ben felt a prickle of fear. Of all people, Jerry O'Connor was the last he wanted to meet. And any hope that he might not be recognized was instantly dashed.

"So it's you again," said O'Connor. "And what new-fangled contraption did ye bring with ye this time?"

Dan Frisbee scowled at Ben. "I thought you said you didn't know any glassworkers."

"I don't know him very well," Ben said stiffly. Nor ever would, if he could help it, he added to himself.

Frisbee looked from one to the other. Ben held his breath. Would O'Connor's remark keep him from being hired? Suddenly he knew how desperately he wanted the job, and just how much he needed that five dollars a week.

"All right, O'Connor, you can go." Frisbee nodded in dismissal.

O'Connor left the shovel standing in the trough and walked off with an indolent air to the door at the side of the room. As he opened it Ben felt a rush of hot air and caught a glimpse of the fiery activity of the glasshouse, where men and boys moved swiftly around, bearing their long iron rods with brightly glowing blobs of glass on the ends.

The door shut, and Frisbee asked, "Now just what was O'Connor talking about?"

"Back in September I helped Ira Benson bring a machine here that pressed glass," Ben began.

"Was that your first time at the factory?" Frisbee interrupted.

"Yes," Ben said, and clamped his lips shut. He'd prove he could hold his tongue.

"I don't care if Jarves brings in a hundred pressing machines," said Frisbee. "Machines might be a good idea, since they'd use more glass. All I care about is making glass and keeping the mix secret."

So that was why he had asked if Ben could keep his mouth shut.

"Hired a man once," Frisbee went on, "who tried to steal our formulas. Caught him writing in a little book." He frowned dourly. "Mind, you're not to say a word to anybody about what you do or see here. Understand?"

"Yes, sir." No doubt about it, Frisbee was deadly serious.

"All right, now. Take off your coat and get to work.

I want you to stir this trough of mix until it's all one color."

Ben hung his coat on a nail and went to work. Although the contents of the trough were dry and powdery, they were not light. He began at one end and shoveled from the bottom, turning gray granules over upon red powder, and white sand upon yellow. When he had worked his way down one side he went back up the other, digging into the mass with rapid thrusts. Soon his shoulders and arms were aching. The mixture was still streaked. This wasn't going to be a quick job. He'd need endurance more than speed. At a slower pace he began his second round.

On the other side of the room Frisbee was dipping into bins labelled *Sand, Red lead, Soda, Potash,* and *Cullet,* filling measures and pouring their contents into another trough. He worked with intense concentration, his lips moving soundlessly. Now and then he consulted a sheet of paper.

A score of questions whirled in Ben's mind. What color glass would this combination of dry stuffs make? Why should there be such secrecy about the ingredients of glass? What had happened to the man who had tried to steal the formula? He longed to speak to Frisbee, but the man was so completely absorbed in his task that he dared not.

From time to time men came into the mixing room pulling small high-sided carts. They filled these from a trough which had been mixed previously, drew them into the glasshouse, then shoveled the contents into huge pots set in the massive circular furnace.

Down into the mass of sand and chemicals went Ben's shovel. Up it came, to blend yellow with gray, and red with white. With every move Ben's shoulders grew wearier.

"Try scattering it. You're not spading a garden, you know," Dan Frisbee suggested.

From then on, Ben could see a change. The streaks and pockets of color disappeared, and the mixture was now a light grayish-brown. Frisbee came over, took the shovel, dug down, lifted a handful, squeezed it, squinted at it, and said judiciously, "Not bad for a start."

From other parts of the building came the sound of doors slamming and feet tramping. Through the smudged windows Ben could see men hurrying past.

"You can go now," said Frisbee. "Come back at seven sharp."

Thankfully Ben took his coat and shrugged it on. Frisbee donned his and unlocked the door. As he opened it two men who had been waiting outside came in. The second shift, thought Ben. Both were middle-aged and serious. Frisbee stepped outside, and Ben followed. Behind them came the sound of the door being bolted and locked. Not a word had passed between the men. They must know their work so well there was no need for talk.

Ben hurried through the gray December noon. Soon he had left behind the other workers, scattering to their homes in the factory village, and was passing through the town. He felt different today, as if he no longer belonged wholly to the old part of Sandwich. As he passed

Water Street he saw Emily in the distance walking toward the Academy for the afternoon session. Would she be surprised about his going to work in the factory? he wondered.

When he came within sight of the old silver-shingled homestead he quickened his steps. Ma would probably have dinner ready, and was he ready for it! Only one thing troubled him. How was he going to tell her that he had taken a job at the glass factory? And Grandfather? He could see the old man shaking with wrath at the news.

Karl Gantz

Once indoors, Ben forgot his own problem. Ma was sitting beside the cot in the back room, laying a damp cloth on Karl Gantz's forehead. The man tossed and muttered. Now and then he coughed painfully.

Ma turned around, her eyes filled with anxiety. "See if you can quiet him, Ben, while I put dinner on the table. The poor soul's in a bad way, and I can't seem to do a thing with him."

The cloth had slipped off the sick man's high domed forehead. Ben put his cool hand in its place and almost drew it away again. The man was burning up with fever! With his other hand, still cold from the long walk, he clasped Karl Gantz's fingers. They, too, were hot. The man's eyes opened and he looked inquiringly at Ben.

"You're going to be all right, Mr. Gantz," Ben said. "You're safe here with us, and you've got Ma to take care of you. There isn't a better nurse in Sandwich."

He couldn't tell whether the man understood the words, but he must have sensed the meaning. Some of the fear went out of his eyes and he lay more quietly, his lids closing. Ben replaced the damp cloth and got up.

"It's a wonder that he knows you," said Ma. "Now you sit down and eat your dinner. And then you'd better go for Justin Dow."

A person had to be pretty sick for Ma to send for Dr. Dow. And there was something in the tone of her voice that gave Ben a cold feeling at the pit of his stomach. He had thought he was hungry, but suddenly food seemed no longer appetizing. He pushed back his half-emptied plate, and said, "I'll go along now."

Ben found the doctor poking with his spoon at a dish of cold pudding which his housekeeper had set before him in his gloomy dining room.

"What kind of patient do you have for me today?" he asked. "Is it animal or human?"

"Human, and he has a bad fever."

"Your grandfather?"

"No, a stranger." Ben told of meeting Karl Gantz at the stagecoach, and finding him later by the roadside.

"If ever I have an accident, I hope it's near your place," was the doctor's short comment.

Together they rode to the Tates' in the doctor's chaise. Silently the doctor made his examination, putting his ear down to the patient's chest and listening as he coughed. Gently he pulled up the covers and said to the sick man, "You're in good hands. You have a fine nurse. Just lie still and try to rest."

Karl Gantz tried to speak again, but burst into a paroxysm of coughing. His questioning eyes followed the doctor as he walked into the kitchen.

"Keep him warm, give him plenty of liquids, and try to make him comfortable. There's not much else you can do, Margaret." The doctor's face was grave.

"Does he have consumption?" asked Ma.

Justin Dow nodded. "It's just a matter of time," he said. "There's no telling how long he'll live."

Ma sighed. "The poor creature, so far from his own country. I keep thinking, suppose Cyrus were sick in a foreign land. I hope someone would care for him."

Ben turned his eyes away. If only Ma wouldn't talk as if Pa were still alive. Dr. Dow must feel the same. Ben sensed the concern in his voice as he began, "Now, Margaret—" Then his words trailed off, and he turned to go.

What was left of the afternoon Ben and Ma spent ministering to Karl Gantz. During a quiet moment while the patient dozed, Ben told Ma of his new job. Surprisingly enough, she did not remonstrate.

"I hate to see you burdened with so much responsibility at your age," she said, "but I'm proud to have such a good son." Tears filled her eyes, and she added, "I think you'd better not tell your grandfather. We might have two patients, then, and we have our hands full as it is." She laughed shakily, and Ben thought he had never felt so close to her.

After supper Ben tried to be casual as he picked up his coat and said, "I'll be going along now."

Phoebe let a pile of plates slide into the dishpan with such speed that the soapy water splashed onto the floor. "Ben Tate, are you going out again tonight? You were out just last night!"

"Ben has some business to take care of," Ma said quietly.

"Like seeing Ira, I suppose."

"Now, Phoebe," Ma said warningly.

Ben slipped out the door. He'd have to tell Phoebe or she'd get Grandfather all stirred up. He set out wearily. The walk to the factory seemed longer tonight. Fatigue had swallowed up the excitement he had felt earlier in the day. Last night's exertion of carrying Karl Gantz home had been poor preparation for a long day of toil.

As Ben neared the factory he found himself in a throng of workers who called back and forth as they made their way to the brightly lighted building. Feeling very much an outsider, Ben was hurrying along when a voice just behind him said, "Hey, slow down, can't you?"

Martin O'Connor caught up with Ben. "I hear you got a job."

"In the mixing room," said Ben, surprised at how glad he was to see a familiar face.

"Old Frisbee's not a bad guy," offered Martin. "It's terrible the way he does chatter on, though, enough to deafen you." His face was sober, but the twinkle in his eyes gave him away.

"I'm going to bring some cotton for my ears tomorrow," said Ben, equally serious.

"Good idea," said Martin, and burst out laughing.

As Ben started toward the back of the factory building the wind from the bay struck cold and raw upon him, but he hardly felt it. Old Frisbee a chatterbox! He was almost laughing when he came up to the locked door and found Frisbee waiting for the key to be turned and the other men to make their exit.

The evening passed in a weary blur. Ben had never known the hours from seven to midnight to be so long. His arms were aching appendages that swung and lifted and scattered the new mountain of sand, potash, lime, and lead that filled the bin.

Just when he was ready to drop from exhaustion there came a tapping on the door. Without a word Frisbee put on his coat, Ben did the same, and they went out into the night.

The cold air gave him energy enough to make his way home, and there he pulled off his boots, crawled beneath the covers, clothes and all, and knew nothing until Ma shook him awake in the morning. Then there was another hill of mix to blend.

At noontime, as Ben was walking homeward, Dr. Dow pulled up beside him in his chaise. "Ride along with me, Ben," he invited. "I'm on my way to your house."

"Is Mr. Gantz worse?" The man had been asleep when Ben had left in the morning.

"I don't know, but I thought I'd look in, anyway. Besides, I wanted to talk with you. Are you still selling wood? I could use a cord of stove lengths."

The doctor was trying to be kind, Ben thought. Didn't he realize that anyone passing his house could see that he had enough wood piled in his open shed to last a year?

"I'm working at the glass factory," he said.

"At the glass factory?" repeated the doctor, giving Ben a sharp look. "What kind of work are you doing there?"

"I mix the ingredients for the glass," said Ben, "sand, potash, lime, and red lead." He tried to make it sound important.

"And that involves exactly what?" persisted the doctor.

There was no point in pretending. "Just using a shovel," Ben said defensively.

For a few minutes Dr. Dow drove in silence. His mare's hoofs clip-clopped on the frozen road. Then he asked, "Have you ever thought of becoming a physician?"

"Me—a doctor?" This must be a joke.

"Yes. You've a good mind and a steady hand, and compassion for the sick. I've watched you with that foreign fellow."

"But getting to be a doctor takes time and money."

"I've decided to give you the schooling you need," Justin Dow said, "as if you were my own son. When you're ready, I'll take you on as my assistant, and we can work together until you can carry on alone." His voice was full of confidence.

Ben felt dazed. The offer was so unexpected he could not grasp it. Stalling for time, he asked, "What about Ma? She needs my pay for taxes and food."

The doctor cleared his throat. "Don't worry about her. I've a plan, as soon as your mother gets over this nonsense about your father. In the meantime I could lend her some money."

"She'd never take it. You know how she is."

"I know how dearly she'd love to see her son a physician," said Justin Dow with finality.

It was true. If Ma had been a man, she would have made a first-rate doctor. Nothing would give her more satisfaction and pride than to have Ben practice medicine. Nevertheless, something kept him from accepting the doctor's offer immediately. Was it because Justin Dow seemed so certain that Ben would delightedly and wholeheartedly fall in with his plan? Some inner voice —probably pure cussedness, thought Ben—made him say stiffly, "I'll have to think it over."

"Think it over!" exploded the doctor. "Do you realize what I'm offering you, boy? Your future on a silver platter!"

Perhaps it was the word "boy" that stung Ben. At the factory the clerk had said Frisbee needed a man. With his present responsibilities Ben felt very much a man.

"I can't decide about my whole life in just a few minutes," he said stubbornly, wondering if he sounded as miserable as he felt.

Karl Gantz, when the doctor examined him, was indeed worse. His fever had subsided, but he lay weak and almost lifeless under the patchwork quilts. Only his eyes seemed alive. Now and again he coughed so painfully that Ben could hardly bear to listen.

When Justin Dow and Ma left the small back bedroom, Ben sat down at the sick man's bedside. He picked up the limp fingers and said, "Not feeling so good today, are you? Too bad."

"Nein. Nicht gut," said Karl Gantz in a whisper.

Then he looked around the room as if to make sure no one else was there, fixed his eyes on Ben, and said slowly, *"Wo ist mein Mantel?"*

What was the man talking about?

"I don't understand," Ben said.

"Mantel. Mein Mantel," the man repeated.

A *mantel.* Wasn't a cloak sometimes called a mantle? Ben recalled Ma hanging Karl Gantz's green coat in the entry to the back shed. He went and fetched it.

There was gratitude and relief in the man's eyes. *"Gut,"* he murmured as Ben spread the folds over him. *"Du bist ein guter Mensch."* He patted the coat and sank back, his strength spent. Ben sat beside him, stroking the worn hand, listening to the low voices in the kitchen. He could imagine Ma's pleasure at Dr. Dow's offer. He wished he could feel as happy about the idea. Probably he was just tired and hungry. After dinner he'd lie down for a while. Everything looked better after a good sleep.

But when he woke up the prospect of becoming a doctor seemed no more enticing. And three days later Ben still had not accepted Justin Dow's offer. Ma, as he had expected, was happier than she had been in a long time. She sang as she went about her work, smiling often.

"Justin says you have great aptitude," she said one noontime. "He thinks you should enroll at the Academy for the rest of this year, and then take your medical studies. Have you told the man at the factory that you're leaving?"

"Not yet," said Ben. He felt as if he had stepped on a greased plank and was sliding along, willy-nilly, with no control over his actions. His whole future seemed to be in the hands of Dr. Dow and his mother. He had thought about the prospect day and night, and although his mind told him he would be a thankless fool to reject the doctor's offer, his feelings told him quite the opposite. He was not sure that he wanted to spend his life at sick people's bedsides, prescribing potions or lancing carbuncles, even though his mother considered a physician's the most noble of all callings. And he could not help resenting Dr. Dow's certainty that his offer would be accepted. Most of all he disliked the fact that the doctor treated him as a boy and made plans for him as if he were unable to think for himself.

Perhaps if he talked with Ira he'd feel better. After the noon meal Ben walked over to his friend's shop. There was a fire in the corner hearth, and Ira was sitting before it, carving a duck out of a piece of soft pine.

"Sit thee down and warm thyself," he said. "The wind is raw today."

Ben stretched his legs out to the fire and sniffed the mingled odors of freshly planed wood, linseed oil, and glue. He could feel his taut nerves easing.

"Thee hasn't been by for quite a spell," observed Ira.

"I've got a job at the glass factory," said Ben, unable to keep the pride out of his voice.

"Does thee like the work?"

"I don't mind it now that I'm used to it," said Ben. It was true. In just a week his muscles had grown used to the shoveling. "In fact, it's sort of interesting. I wish Mr. Frisbee would let me measure out a batch sometime."

"What goes into glass?" asked Ira. "I've often wondered."

"First of all there's fourteen hundred pounds of sand, one hundred pounds of soda, and eight hundred pounds of red lead. There's some ash, I can't remember just how much, and cullet, quite a lot of that," said Ben eagerly. "You know what cullet is—broken pieces of glass."

Suddenly he clapped his hand over his mouth. Dan Frisbee had told him never to breathe a word about the mix to anyone, and here, at the very first question, he was telling Ira all he could remember.

"Just forget everything I told you," he begged. "Mr. Frisbee warned me not to talk about my work. I guess every glassmaker has his own special formulas, and they have to be kept secret."

"Don't worry about my telling," said Ira. "I've no head for figures, and besides, I'll never set foot in that place again. I'm surprised that thee went there to work."

"I had to do something," Ben said, "especially now that we've one more person to feed," and launched into the tale of Karl Gantz. He had hated to leave Karl this afternoon. The man seemed weaker, and his eyes had followed Ben with yearning, as if he longed to talk with him.

"What I came about was this plan Dr. Dow has for me," Ben said, and he told Ira the details. "I know I ought to accept his offer and be thankful, but I can't seem to make up my mind."

Ira was silent for a time. "Hast thee taken this matter to the Lord?" he asked.

Ben was embarrassed. "I hadn't thought of that," he said.

"Thee might lay it in His hands for a while," Ira offered. "It is possible that He might show thee the way."

"You mean with a pillar of fire or something?" Ben could almost see a fiery beacon leading him to the Academy and Dr. Dow's front parlor.

Ira chuckled. "It is possible He might employ some sign, although hardly such a spectacle. Thee isn't quite as important as the children of Israel, although at times thee may think so."

Ben laughed. Already he felt better. "Do you think I'm crazy not to jump at the chance to be a doctor?"

"I think thee needs more time to think it over. And I know thee likes to make up thy own mind."

That night in bed Ben remembered Ira's words. He had not said a prayer for a long time. Perhaps he should turn the problem over to God. He was wondering how to phrase his request when he fell asleep, a picture forming in his mind of himself, small as a puppet, standing on the outstretched hands of the Lord. Strangely enough, the hands, gigantic in size, were the same as Karl Gantz's, calloused and scarred.

The next day, when he awoke, Ben felt as confused as ever. Just before he left the house, his mother asked, "Have you given notice yet?"

He had all he could do to keep from shouting at her.

"No, not yet," he said. Inwardly he was fuming. Couldn't she leave him alone?

Day by day Karl Gantz grew weaker. His eyes sank far back in his head, and the skin stretched taut across his cheekbones. Still he clung to a feeble thread of life.

One afternoon, when Ben came into the back bedroom, he saw that Karl had brightened. He smiled at Ben, and there was color in his cheeks. When Ben sat at his bedside, the sick man held out the dark-green coat and picked with a ridged fingernail at certain threads until he had opened a seam. He pushed the material aside, disclosing a folded piece of paper. With trembling hands he drew it forth and opened it, holding it close to his eyes to read.

Then he folded it again with a deep sigh, touched his lips to it for an instant, and handed it to Ben.

"Dieses ist für dich. Bewahre es wohl."

The paper was worn and spotted and blackened on the edges. Obviously Karl Gantz considered it of great value. The brown eyes willed Ben to open it. Carefully he smoothed out the creases.

The paper was covered with handwriting in faded ink. Ben peered at it closely. He had never seen letters formed as these were. He strove to cover his confusion and smiled.

"It's very nice," he said politely. "Thank you, Mr. Gantz."

Karl put his finger to his lips as if to signify the need for secrecy, then put his hand inside his nightshirt.

"You want me to hide it?" Ben asked. "All right, I'll

put it in my pocket." He slid the creased folds deep down in his shirt pocket.

The German smiled and nodded. *"Schönstes Rubinglas,"* he said, *"mit Gold gemacht."*

When Ben stepped into the small bedroom before leaving for work that evening, Karl Gantz was aleep. He must be dreaming happily, Ben thought, for his face was serene.

But when Ben got home just after midnight, the large lamp was burning on the sitting-room table and his mother met him at the door. Her expression told him what had happened even before she spoke.

"Mr. Gantz died in his sleep, probably soon after you left. I went in to see him about nine o'clock, and knew at once that he had gone. Poor man, so far from home, with none of his own near him."

Hasty Words

Few mourners accompanied the body of Karl Gantz to the old burying ground by the millpond the following afternoon. The minister and Grandfather led the cortege, then came Ma and Phoebe, Ira and Dr. Dow, and at the very end, Ben. The interment was to be in the Tate lot. The hospitality given during Karl Gantz's lifetime should be continued after his death, Ma said.

As he stood beside the gaping hole in the cemetery, the raw wind gnawing at his back, Ben was overcome with sorrow for the stranger who had journeyed far only to meet violence and death.

When the last prayer had been offered, Ben turned to Ma. "I'd like to put up a stone marker for Mr. Gantz as soon as I get some money ahead."

"You ought to buy one for your father first," said the doctor, looking significantly at a marble headstone nearby, with the words *Lost at Sea* carved at the top.

Ma's face took on the stricken, pinched look she had worn in the days immediately after the sinking of the *Orion*. She wrapped her cloak tightly around her and said, "Come along, Phoebe, we'd best go home. It's too cold to stand around talking."

Ben wished the doctor would mind his own business. Ever since he had offered to help Ben it had seemed as if he were trying to run his life. Ben would like nothing better than to walk away from them all—run, even. Not just from the cemetery, but from the town itself.

Beside him Grandfather stumbled on the uneven ground. Ben took his arm, and from the way the older man leaned on him, Ben knew that he would have to steady him all the way home. Resentfully he slowed his pace to Grandfather's plodding steps. There was only one thing to be thankful for. Dr. Dow had not asked him this afternoon when he was going to give up his job at the glassworks.

Ben was still undecided about what he should do. He knew that Ma thought he should accept the doctor's help, and was sure that Grandfather agreed. He suspected that Ira was of the same mind. And Phoebe's eagerness was sickening.

"Just think of having a doctor for a brother! I'll be able to hold my head up with anyone—even the Jarveses. And I can have as many pairs of shoes as I want. Oh, Ben, it will be wonderful!"

After he had filled the wood box, fed the animals, and had his own supper, it was a relief to go out of the house into the quiet dark. He stepped out with long strides and suddenly realized that he was looking forward to the evening's work. There was something satisfying about blending the mix for the glass. It had to be done just right or the materials would not melt properly. Dan

Frisbee's arm had been paining last night. Ben wondered if it was any worse. If so, he might need help in
measuring out the materials for the mix.

When Ben met Dan at the mixing room door and saw
that he was cradling one arm in the other, he felt wicked
about being so elated. He tried not to be too eager when
the older man said, once they were inside, "You might
give me a hand over here, Tate. I could have asked for
another man tonight, but I'm sure you'll do a good job."

Another *man.* That was one thing Ben liked about
working at the glass factory. Not once had he been re-
ferred to as a boy. He was doing a man's job, and he was
considered one. Feeling inches taller, he said, "Just tell
me what you want done, Mr. Frisbee."

The older man drew a crisp sheet of paper from his
pocket. "Mr. Jarves gave me this as I was passing the
office this noon. It's a new shade of purple glass he wants
to try out."

"Mr. Jarves is back!"

Mr. Frisbee glanced up in mild surprise at the aston-
ishment in Ben's voice. "Yes, he came in on yesterday's
packet." He looked at the paper. "Now you'll need
eighty pounds of sand for a starter. Measure that out
first."

Ben walked over to the box and began shoveling the
sand. Would the men in the glasshouse turn on Mr.
Jarves as they had before? Was it safe for him to return
to Sandwich? Dan Frisbee said he had been in his office.
Evidently Mr. Jarves felt that the danger had passed or
he would not have returned.

When the sand had been measured into the trough,

Dan Frisbee said, "Just take a look at these figures, will you? I can't tell whether this is an eight or a three. The light's not so good here as it used to be."

Ben peered at the paper with a strange feeling that he had seen it before. But that was impossible. Mr. Jarves had given it to Dan Frisbee only that noon.

"It's a three," he said. "Shall I put in thirty pounds of red lead?"

"Go ahead," said Frisbee.

While Ben shoveled the red lead out of the box into the measure and turned it into the trough he tried to remember where he had seen such a piece of paper before. The placement of the figures and the handwriting evoked a hazy memory. Suddenly it came to him. The paper Karl Gantz had given him! Though worn and creased, it resembled the formula Dan Frisbee held in his hand.

Karl Gantz had been a glassmaker, Ben was sure. He had brought a glassmaker's tools with him in his satchel. And he had asked to be directed to the glass factory and Mr. Jarves. Could the paper he had given Ben be a formula for making glass? Might he have been about to sell that formula to Deming Jarves?

Ben was so excited that he almost lost count of the amount of red lead he had put into the trough. Resolutely he concentrated on the business in hand. He would have to wait until he got home to examine the paper. He put his hand to his pocket, and felt nothing. For a moment he panicked. Had he lost the paper? Then he looked at his shirt. It was brown. The one he had worn yesterday was blue. Ma must have taken it to wash. He was so upset he almost dropped his shovel. Suppose Ma had washed the shirt, and the paper with it? Once it struck the water, the writing would be illegible.

The thought was so unnerving that Ben broke out in a sweat. How could he have been such a dunce as not to realize the value of Karl's gift? Dan Frisbee's flat tones brought him back to the task before him.

"Now put in thirty pounds of cullet," he said.

Ben gave himself a mental kick. If he didn't keep his mind on his job, he'd lose it. He settled down to measuring.

When all the ingredients had been put into the trough, Dan Frisbee said, "We'll mix the purple now. Mr. Jarves wants it put to melt tonight."

Ben turned and scattered vigorously. If he worked hard, Mr. Frisbee might call on him again to make up the mixture. After an hour's work Frisbee went to the door of the glasshouse, opened it, and shouted for the trucks. In a few minutes two men appeared, each pulling a cart. One of the men was Jerry O'Connor.

He peered at the mixture. "Hmmm. Looks different from the usual. What did you put into it?"

Ben looked toward Frisbee. He appeared not to have heard the question but was rubbing his shoulder.

"It's all right for you to tell me. I work here," said O'Connor in a wheedling tone.

"Why don't you ask Mr. Frisbee? He knows more about it than I do," said Ben.

Frisbee looked up. "Better get those trucks loaded," he said. O'Connor spat and began to shovel.

Once he had left the factory, Ben couldn't get home

fast enough. The house was dark except for a pink glow where the drafts of the stove were cracked open. He lit a candle and went up to his room. The shirt was not on the chair where he had flung it last night. Had Ma hung it on the hook in the corner? No.

He went downstairs and saw in a corner of the kitchen the big wooden washtub, resting on two saw-horses. He held the candle over its soggy contents and saw with a sinking heart the unmistakable folds of his blue shirt. He set the candle down and pulled at the shirt until he found the pocket. His exploring fingers felt nothing in it, not even a sodden wad. Ma must have taken the paper out.

Where had she put it? He began to search the kitchen. Not on the table, not on the shelf between the windows. Not beside the clock. He tried to put himself in Ma's place as she got the washing ready.

He went over to the pump. She would have filled the bucket of water here and taken it to the tub. He held the candle near the narrow shelf above the sink. A mug, a few buttons, an old saucer with a piece of soap, and ah! What was that under the saucer? He lifted it up and could have wept for joy. There was the paper, just as Karl Gantz had given it to him, except that one edge was wet from moisture trapped under the dish.

By the light of the candle Ben examined the paper. The last line was a meaningless smudge where water had dissolved the ink.

Once more he was struck by the resemblance between this handwritten page and the formula prepared by Mr. Jarves. There was list of what must be ingredients. The words, however, baffled him. Not only were they in another language, but the formation of the letters was unlike any handwriting Ben had ever seen.

Suddenly very tired, he yawned. There was nothing more he could do about the paper tonight. Somehow he would find a way to decipher it.

Stumbling with weariness, he went upstairs and undressed. The paper he put carefully in a small sea chest that Ira had made for his tenth birthday.

As his head touched the pillow Ben remembered his talk with Ira. He had given his problem into the Lord's hands. Again he had a vision of himself, small as a puppet, standing on the gigantic hands that were scarred and calloused like Karl's. This paper with the formula —could it be a sign from the Lord as to what he must do? Surely it did not point toward his becoming a physician. He was not positive that the Lord meant him to keep on with his job at the glassworks, but that was the only way he could figure out what the paper meant. Perhaps he could ask Mr. Jarves about it. He drifted off to sleep.

Getting to see Mr. Jarves was not as easy as Ben had thought it would be. He left the house early the next day, Karl Gantz's formula wrapped in a clean sheet of paper, carefully stowed in his pocket. When he knocked at the office door, the sour-faced man informed him that Mr. Jarves was not accustomed to come so early.

At noontime Ben tried again. This time he was told that Mr. Jarves had gone to the inn for his dinner. Ben made a special trip to the office in the afternoon, but learned that Mr. Jarves was taking an important visitor through the factory.

The following day he went through much the same process, only to meet with the same disappointment. And the third day he was told that Mr. Jarves had returned to his home in Boston.

In desperation Ben showed the paper to Dan Frisbee, who examined it carefully and listened to Ben's account of how it had come into his hands.

"It looks like a formula for glass, but it could be almost anything. You might ask O'Connor. He worked in Pennsylvania with some Germans once."

Jerry O'Connor was the last person Ben would tell about Karl Gantz's gift. He couldn't forget his suspicion that it was Jerry O'Connor and Steve Tully he had seen coming from the highway the night that Karl Gantz had been struck and left in the ditch to die. There was no proof that they were the ones who had attacked him, but Ben had a strong feeling that they had been up to no good that dark night.

Ben went home at noontime, discouraged. He'd have to wait for Mr. Jarves to come back to Sandwich and then try again to see him. Whether he would be successful was another matter.

That afternoon Ben was in the barn, cleaning out Star's stall, when Dr. Dow drove into the yard. He seemed to find a good many reasons for stopping by nowadays.

Ben finished his work, hung the pitchfork on the wall, and went into the house. He could hear Ma and the doctor talking in the sitting room.

"Come in, dear. Justin wants to see you," his mother called. Her voice had a new liveliness.

Ben washed his hands, taking his time. He was sure of what Dr. Dow had come to discuss, but he was not quite sure how he would answer him.

As Ben stepped into the cosy room, its bay window banked in geraniums, the doctor inquired, "Are you almost through with that foolishness of working at the factory, boy?"

The phrasing of the question stung Ben to anger. "I'm not going to quit. I like it there, and I'm going to stay."

"Do you plan to shovel sand the rest of your life?" Dr. Dow asked.

"It isn't just sand," said Ben. "There's lime and red lead and other things, too. I don't plan to stay in the mixing room forever. I might start a glassworks of my own someday."

He stopped in consternation. He had intended to say something about appreciating the doctor's kindness, but not wanting to be indebted to such an extent. Instead he had blurted out a lot of bragging nonsense. The idea of starting a glassworks had entered his head only a minute ago. If the doctor hadn't called him "boy," he might not have lost his temper and gone on and on like a fool.

Ma was looking at him strangely, disappointment and shock clear upon her face. The doctor was plainly offended. He rose stiffly and said, "Good afternoon, Margaret. I can see that I'm wasting my time here. It's a puzzle to me how a sensible woman like you could have raised so shortsighted a son. I fear you'll both regret his decision."

He passed Ben with a cold stare and let himself out the front door. Ma put both hands up to her face. Ben stood miserable and silent for a few minutes.

"I didn't mean to say all that," he said at last. "I don't know what got into me."

"I thought you *wanted* to be a doctor," Ma said, her voice muffled. "It was my greatest hope for you."

"I can't stand the way Dr. Dow thinks all his ideas are right, and mine are wrong," Ben stormed.

"Well, I don't like the idea of your working in that factory, either," said Ma.

"You like the money I earn well enough," said Ben.

Ma dropped her hands and gave him one look. Ben had never seen her face like that before, with hurt and pain written on it.

Choking with anger and disgust for his words, Ben left. As he passed through the kitchen he caught up an old jacket and rammed his arms into it, then hurried out the door. Outside he started to run, heading for the shore. He did not stop until he had reached the dunes.

As he topped the most seaward rise the strong east wind, frigid from the North Atlantic, caught at his throat. Below him breakers plunged shoreward with a bleak ferocity that matched his own. Waves like these had robbed him of his father.

He half ran, half slid down the steep incline to the beach, then marched along its wet length, his mood as stormy as the gray clouds above. What had caused him to speak in such a way to his mother? There was no one in the world he loved more, no one in the world he wanted less to injure. Yet he had hurt her cruelly. He would have given anything to take back his words. But nothing would erase them from her mind—or from his.

Sheer exhaustion drove him home. He let himself in the back door, thankful to find the kitchen empty, and went up the stairs to his room. Surprisingly, sleep came to him. He woke to Phoebe's knock and rose, half awake and fully miserable.

Supper was a silent meal. Phoebe made a few attempts at chatter, looked fearfully from her mother to Ben, and not liking what she saw, cleared her plate swiftly. She followed Ben out the back door, as he had suspected she would, and said, "What's wrong, Ben? Has something terrible happened?"

"I'm not going to be a doctor," he said flatly.

"Oh, Ben," she wailed, "you've got to. I've told all my friends."

Silly little fool, he thought. Did she expect him to plan his life just to suit her?

"I've got to get to work," he said roughly, and hurried down the path, so filled with misery he hardly knew where he was going. The walk through the cold air was bracing. He felt almost normal when he reached the mixing room. To his disappointment, Dan Frisbee's shoulder was better, and Ben was put back to his old job. He began to wonder if the doctor was right, and he would spend the rest of his life shoveling sand.

That night as Ben trudged home he saw a light shining in the graveyard. What would anyone be doing there at midnight? Despite his fatigue he cut behind the gristmill and along Grove Street. As he approached the cemetery he heard a grating sound.

Keeping in the shadow of the stone wall that bordered the burying ground, Ben drew near the light. It came from a lantern set on a stone in his own family's lot. Next to it was a gaping hole, a pile of earth, and a coffin—over which two men were bent, their faces hidden in shadow.

While Ben watched, numb with horror, one of the men thrust the blade of a shovel under the lid and pried it open. The other began fumbling at the body within.

"It must be somewhere on him." The voice was so muffled Ben could hardly make out the words. "I heard him say *Gold,* plain as could be, when he was talking with Mr. Jarves's clerk."

"If there's gold on him, I'll find it," said the other.

Ben sprang to his feet, picking up one of the heavy stones that formed the wall.

"Grave robbers!" he shouted. "Get away from that coffin!" He threw the rock with all his force at the taller of the men and heard him grunt as it hit his shoulder.

The shorter man gave a cry and set off at a run, followed by his companion. Ben was left alone in the night with the lantern and the open coffin.

Trembling, he held the light near the body of Karl Gantz. The face was still peaceful, the clothing undisturbed. Ben pushed the lid down and with a rock hammered the nails into place. There was heavy rope lying on the ground, and he used it to lower the coffin. Then he took the shovel and filled in the grave.

When he had finished, he walked to the edge of the

pond and threw the lantern and shovel far out into the water. Never again would they be used for so ugly a deed.

As he walked past the newly filled grave toward home, tears were streaming down his face. If there was any more sorrow and cruelty in the world, he didn't want to know about it. All he wanted to know was the identity of the men who had tried to rob the body of Karl Gantz. Were they the same ruffians who had struck him down on the highway? Whoever they were, he hoped they would meet their just desserts, and soon.

German Lessons

Days passed in a dull, joyless pattern. Mealtime, which had always been a pleasure, not only for the good food but for the exchange of news, became an occasion that Ben dreaded. Food tasted sour when it was curdled with resentment and regret. If his body had not needed the nourishment, he would have skipped meals altogether. He dawdled on the way home, or found tasks to keep him busy in the barn until the others had finished eating, and then had a cold meal by himself. While eating he kept his head down and avoided Ma's eyes as she worked around the kitchen.

Instead of proudly handing over his weekly five dollars and feeling rewarded by Ma's smile, Ben now placed the money beside the clock without a word. When Ma announced one day in February that she had paid the yearly tax of $38.28, he hardly felt elated. His money had kept their home safe, but the victory was meaningless without Ma's love and understanding.

Something about the situation made Ben shrink from

any human contact. Even Honor's overtures he re-buffed.

When she said, "I think you have a right to decide what you want to do with your life, Ben," he whirled on her and stormed, "Why don't you mind your own business?" For days afterward her bewildered eyes haunted him.

Each day he walked back and forth from home to the glassworks, his eyes on the ground, so that he would not see anyone and have to speak. All the world seemed to be against him. Why should he pretend that he was glad to see people or greet them?

He learned that Mr. Jarves had again returned to Sandwich, but made no effort to see him. The paper of Karl Gantz's was probably worthless. Besides, Mr. Jarves couldn't be bothered to see a mere hired hand from the mixing room.

One noontime as he plodded his sullen way home-ward through freshly fallen snow he heard a voice behind calling his name. He pretended not to hear and kept on walking. Quick footsteps sounded beside him, and a bright face peered up into his own.

"You must be thinking about something very interesting," Emily said. "I wanted to ask you how Star is. I haven't seen you driving him lately."

"I can't leave him standing outside the glassworks for hours at a time," Ben said gruffly.

"Of course not. He'd catch cold in this weather."

Ben slanted a look at her. Was she interested only in Star? Didn't she care that he was working at the factory?

"Nobody drives to the glassworks except Mr. Jarves," he said.

"I suppose you will when you get to be as important as he is," Emily said in a matter-of-fact manner.

"I'm certainly not very important now," said Ben. "All I do is mix the stuff that makes glass."

"That sounds awfully important to me," said Emily. "There wouldn't be any factory or any jobs for anybody if you didn't do your work."

Ben looked at her in amazement. She was right. If he and Dan Frisbee and the men on the other shift should quit, the whole factory would have to shut down.

Emily gave a skip. "Oh, bother, my shoelace is untied. Will you hold my books for a minute, please?" She handed him the armful and bent down.

Ben glanced at the books. On top was a German grammar. Between its pages lay a large sheet of paper covered with neat handwriting. There was something strange about the letters. Ben looked at them closely. They were formed in the same manner as those on the paper Karl Gantz had given him!

When Emily had straightened up, Ben pointed to the sheet. "What's this about?" he demanded.

"That's the story of the phoenix, the anxient Egyptian bird that was supposed to live for five hundred years, then was consumed in fire, and rose in youthful freshness from its own ashes." Emily threw up her arms as if they were wings. "Isn't that exciting?"

Ben couldn't help smiling. Emily could make anything seem exciting. "A phoenix sounds like a pretty queer bird," he said, "but I'm a lot more curious about the way you've written about it."

"Oh, you mean the German script," said Emily. "It's fun to do."

"Can you actually read and write German?" Ben demanded.

"Of course. Can't you? Oh, I forgot, German isn't taught in the town school."

Ben took a deep breath. Life had been so bleak for so long he could hardly believe in this piece of good fortune. "Could you teach me to read German script?" he asked, his heart in his mouth lest she refuse.

"I guess I could. I save all my papers for when I'm a teacher." Suddenly she clapped her hands. "Oh, Ben, you'll be my first pupil. I can practice on you."

"When may I have my first lesson, teacher?" he asked.

"Not tonight, because you work then. And not this afternoon, because school doesn't get out until four and I may have to stay to help correct papers. That's how I earn part of my tuition, you know."

"Well, it was just an idea," said Ben. He might have known that the idea of his learning German was too good to be true. Everything had gone wrong lately. He was a failure, and he might as well face it.

"What time do you have to be at work at night?" asked Emily.

"Seven," Ben said glumly.

"Why don't you come to my house a little before six? We'd have almost an hour then."

"What about your father's supper?"

"He has it at five. The store's very quiet then because most of the women are home cooking."

"You're sure it will be all right?" Ben asked, still doubtful.

"Of course. Why don't we start today? I'll have everything ready," Emily said.

Ben lifted the brass knocker on the Griswold's front door at five minutes before six. He was greeted by a formidable woman with a fresh pink-and-white complexion, an aquiline nose, and a cloud of white hair piled high.

"Good evening, young man," she said frostily.

"Good evening," Ben mumbled, conscious of his work clothes and snowy boots. He ran one foot and then the other over the snow scraper at the edge of the steps.

Emily suddenly appeared beside the woman. "Aunt Cassie, this is Ben Tate," she said. "He's the pupil I told you about."

"He seems rather old to be just beginning German," the woman commented. She extended her hand. "I am Mrs. Humphrey, Mr. Griswold's sister."

Ben took her hand, hoping his own was clean.

"Let me have your coat, Ben, and then we'll go into the sitting room," Emily said. "I've lighted a fire in the fireplace."

"At my home in Boston, when Mr. Humphrey was alive, we had stoves in every room on the first floor, and in the upstairs hall," the aunt announced.

"You must have burned a lot of wood," said Ben.

Aunt Cassie sniffed. "Wood? Dear me, no. Mr. Humphrey would burn nothing but coal. He believed in all the latest things, poor dear." She drew a lace-edged handkerchief from her bosom and dabbed at her eyes.

"You may sit here, Ben," said Emily, "next to me where we can both look at the book." She glanced at her aunt. "Would you rather we went into the kitchen, Aunt Cassie, so you could read without being disturbed?"

"No, indeed. I'll just sit here and do my tatting."

"The first thing is to learn the alphabet in German," said Emily, suddenly very business-like. "It looks the same as ours, but it sounds different. Now say after me: *ah, bay, tse, day, ay, eff, ghay, hah, ee, yot, kah—*"

At first Ben felt silly repeating the strange sounds, especially with Mrs. Humphrey sitting there, stabbing with the point of her silver shuttle at the fine thread. Soon he became so engrossed in getting the letters right when Emily pointed to them that he almost forgot her aunt.

At a quarter to seven the factory bell rang out. How had fifty minutes passed so quickly? Ben felt as if he had just stepped inside the door.

"Oh, dear, it's time for you to go," said Emily. "Why don't you take this along, Ben? It's the English letters and the German script side by side. Maybe you'll have a chance to memorize some of them before tomorrow's lesson."

Ben covered the distance from the Griswold house to the glassworks in double-quick time. Although the snow squeaked beneath his feet and the ruts at the corner of Dock Lane were frozen solid, he didn't feel as cold as usual. Probably that was because of the fire in the hearth at Emily's house. He felt warm clear through.

As he was nearing the glassworks he saw a familiar figure ahead. "Hi, Martin," he called out cheerily.

Martin stopped and waited for him. "Well, what happened to you?" he asked. "Did you get a raise?"

"Whatever gave you that idea?"

"Something good must have happened," said Martin. "This is the first time in weeks you've even looked at me. I was beginning to think you'd turned into a second Frisbee."

In spite of himself, Ben laughed. "Say, how did that batch of purple glass work out? Did your shop like it?" he asked.

"The color was fine, but the glass was ambitty," said Martin. He chuckled. "Is that a new one for you? It means the glass won't work up well."

"What was wrong with it?" Ben asked. "Was it too thin, or too thick?"

"It was just ambitty," said Martin. "It wouldn't do what you expected. It acted queer, like people do sometimes."

"Are you trying to tell me that I'm ambitty?" Ben asked with a grin.

"No," said Martin. "I was thinking of my uncle Jerry. He went off last night and didn't come back. I found this note on the table this morning." He held out a scrap of paper.

Ben read the penciled scrawl at a glance: *Martin— You have got a good job now, so I am going off with Steve. We heard about a glassworks in New Jersey that*

*pays big. You can have these tools. The man that owned
them don't need them no more.*

So Jerry O'Connor had left Sandwich. Ben felt a sense
of relief. The factory would be a better place without
him and his friend Steve Tully. Ben looked at Martin,
thinking to see the same reaction. But the young man
was staring at the ground.

"He didn't want me to go with him," he said sadly.

"At least now you won't have to look after him," Ben
offered.

Martin regarded him stonily. "Now I've got nobody."

"Where are the tools he left for you?" Ben asked.

"Here," said Martin, drawing from beneath his arm a
bundle wrapped in a piece of bright cloth.

Ben drew back in consternation. That cloth—he had
seen it before! Karl Gantz had wrapped his tools in just
such a colorful material the day Ben had helped him
pick them up after his fall from the stagecoach. Jerry
O'Connor and Steve Tully must have attacked the German that dark night and stolen his valise, thinking to
find in it the gold Jerry had overheard Karl speak of to
Mr. Jarves's clerk. Here was evidence that they had
robbed him, and some day Ben would find proof that
they had attempted to rob his grave.

Ben was about to blurt out his conclusions when Martin spoke. He had the pucella in his hand and was moving it in the air as if he were shaping a vase with the
tool's two long prongs.

"At least he thought enough of me to leave me these
tools," he said softly. "They must have belonged to
some friend of his."

Ben choked back a denial. Telling the truth now would do no good to anyone. The disclosure of Jerry O'Connor's misdeeds could not help Karl Gantz, and it would hurt Martin deeply.

Martin was holding the calipers in his calloused fingers. A memory of Karl's hands came to Ben's mind.

"The man who owned those tools would be glad to know that they'll be well used," he said.

"I'll use them, all right," said Martin. "I've been waiting for a chance to borrow the gaffer's tools to make some offhand pieces in between shifts. Now I can use my own."

The following week when Ben was in the stock room getting a new shovel, the stockman complained, "It's hard to keep track of tools. I'm short one shovel and a lantern. Jerry O'Connor signed for them, but he's left town. Probably I'll never get them back."

Probably he never will, thought Ben, unless the pond runs dry. He felt no anger at the knowledge, only bitter disgust. Martin was too good a fellow to be burdened with the knowledge of his uncle's grave-robbing attempt.

That noon Ben invited Martin to come home with him for dinner, and Martin accepted.

The next morning Dan Frisbee had orders to mix a trial batch of a peacock-blue shade.

"Go down to the pot room and fetch me a monkey," he ordered.

Ben thought his ears must be deceiving him. "Fetch a *what?*" he asked.

"A monkey pot, a little one that sits on top of the regular ones," Frisbee said.

Ben could smell the earthy damp of the pot room the minute he opened the door. At one side of the room was a trough filled with a mass of wet brown clay which a man was treading with bare feet. Nearby another man was rolling clay into cylinders about four inches long and two inches thick. And farther on, a third workman was applying the rolls to the walls of what appeared to be half a hogshead made of clay. Ranged about the room were clay pots in various stages of manufacture, and in one corner a dozen or so small clay containers.

The third workman looked up. "Want a monkey pot?"

"That's right," said Ben.

"Take the one farthest to the right," the man said. "It's cured long enough."

To Ben's delight, when he returned to the mixing room, Dan Frisbee let him assist in mixing the trial batch. The quantities seemed very small after the scores of pounds he was accustomed to handling. All the more reason for accuracy, he reasoned, and he worked with meticulous care.

In the days that followed there was a sudden surge of activity in every department of the glassworks. Mr. Jarves had brought from Boston enough orders to keep the factory working at top capacity for months. There were more new colors to mix. And most amazing of all, the carpenters were at work on another pressing machine, made according to plans drawn by Mr. Jarves.

"Isn't Mr. Jarves afraid that the men will smash this

machine, too?" Ben asked Martin one noon as they left the factory together.

"He's been careful to let everybody know that all the orders he's taken will keep every man working full time," said Martin. "They're no longer afraid that they'll lose their jobs."

"He told them that before," Ben said.

"They thought he was just talking," said Martin. "This time he's proved to them that they'll have plenty of work by having all the orders tacked up in the glass-house. And every time new orders come in, he puts those up, too. The men can see how much work there is to be done, and they don't worry."

Ben whistled. Mr. Jarves was pretty smart.

The next day after work Ben went over to the carpenter shop. It seemed years rather than months ago that he and Ira had brought the pressing machine there. He inspected the new device critically. It was a replica of Ira's design. Again he had to admire Mr. Jarves. How many men could study a combination of levers and plungers and draw an exact reproduction from memory?

One day when Ben reported for work, he found another man in the mixing room with Frisbee. A serious, gray-mustached person, he was a close-mouthed as Frisbee and, Ben soon learned, a capable worker. Had the new man been hired to replace Ben? He worked harder than ever. He'd show Dan Frisbee that youthful muscles were better than old.

The following day one of the men assigned to wheel the trucks of mix to the furnace was absent.

"Tate, you take care of number-two truck," Frisbee said.

Now he'd have a chance to fill the pot and observe the melting. His spirits lifted, Ben thrust his shovel into the mix and started filling the box on wheels.

When it was ready, he pulled it into the glasshouse, following the number-one truck. As always, the heat of the room almost stifled him. When the other man opened the metal door at the mouth of the pot, Ben couldn't help drawing back. His face felt as if it were seared.

He watched while the filler lifted a shovel and deftly shot its contents into the mouth of the pot. Again and again he repeated the motions, until he had emptied the truck. Then he stood aside and gestured to Ben to discharge his load.

Even a few feet made a difference in the degree of heat, Ben learned. He jammed his shovel into the mix, lifted it, and in his haste, hit the edge of the opening. The contents scattered on the floor.

"Don't take so much at once," said the filler.

The next time, Ben scooped up less than a shovelful. He kept his hand steady and took careful aim for the opening. There! He had got it in. Once more he took a small amount, raised his arms, and let the mix fly into the opening.

"I guess you've got the knack," said the man. "Get a move on. You can't let the furnace cool off."

Cool off! The workman must be joking. Ben turned his head, a smile ready.

"Hurry up!" said the filler. "A few degrees makes a

difference in the glass. You don't want to ruin a batch."
He was deadly serious.

Frowning, Ben put all his effort into transferring the
mix from the truck to the pot. There was a trick to sliding the stuff off before the shovel got too hot to hold.

For three days Ben worked as a temporary filler. On
the fourth day Dan Frisbee said, "You can have the job
steady if you want it. Pays fifty cents more a week."

"I'll take it," said Ben. More than the extra pay at-
tracted him. He'd been watching the glass blowers and
their assistants while he pulled his truck from the mixing room to the furnace. More and more he was becoming fascinated by the mysteries of glassmaking.

The Formula

German was hard to learn, but not nearly so difficult as Ben had anticipated. Emily expressed amazement at his progress.

"You're going ahead faster than we did in the Academy," she said. "You must be very smart."

"The German is the only thing I have to study," said Ben. "I don't need to divide my time between algebra and geography and literature."

"But you have to spend a lot of time at work," retorted Emily. "I still think you learn very quickly."

Ben accepted her praise thankfully. Studying German was about all he had to do after he had finished his chores at home. When he had filled the wood box and taken care of the animals, there was little else to occupy him.

Ma was busy with sewing these days. She had told friends and neighbors that she would do dressmaking, and the sitting room was filled with feminine garments in some stage of assembly, a sleeve here, a ruffle there, or a collar pinned to the arm of a rocker. Months ago Ben would have settled down and talked with Ma during the long afternoons. Now he went to his room and concentrated on German nouns and verbs.

There was no heat in the bedrooms except the little that came up from the kitchen and sitting-room stoves. Ben put on extra socks and a heavy jacket, but he had to stand up now and then and swing his arms and legs in an effort to get warm. Worse than the physical cold was the icy wall that separated him from Ma.

The winter passed, bleak and cheerless except for the daily study period at the Griswold house. Ben looked forward all day to the hour he would spend with Emily. She was cheerful and so bright and quick it was a pleasure to be with her. He was sorry that he was not able to pay her. He explained painfully that every penny must go to Ma.

Emily threw up her hands in protest. "I couldn't possibly take money from you. Think of the practice you're giving me. When I apply for a teaching position, I can say that I have tutored a young man. Now, how do you say, 'The grass is green'?"

"Das Gras ist grün," Ben said, grinning. "That's too easy. Let's get into the next lesson."

Now and then Ben took Karl Gantz's formula from the small sea chest on his bureau and examined it. Here and there he could recognize a word. On another sheet of paper he drew lines and set down the English translation in the approximate position of the German sentences.

Spring came reluctantly. The wind off the ocean carried a chill, but the grass grew green, buds reddened on the maples, and in damp hollows mayflowers showed their tender pink.

At the factory the new pressing machine was moved into the glasshouse, and men were assigned to operate it. Each time he wheeled a truckload of mix to the furnace, Ben watched to see how the machine was working. Whenever molten glass was put into the mold, a cloud of smoke arose. Ben was not surprised to hear one morning that the machine had broken down.

That noon, after work, Ben stopped at the office. "I'd like to see Mr. Jarves," he said to the dour man behind the rail.

"He's busy," said the clerk. "State your business, and I'll tell it to him when he's free."

"It's about the machine—" Ben began.

"The pressing machine has broken down," said the man with finality.

"I have an idea of how to fix it," said Ben.

"Do you work on the machine?"

"No, I'm a filler."

"Stick to your job, then." The man picked up a pen.

Just then an inner door opened, and Mr. Jarves appeared. "Did I hear something about the pressing machine?" he asked as he came into the outer office. Giving Ben a keen look, he exclaimed, "Upon my word, it's young Tate. Did you want to see me?"

"Yes," said Ben, "if you're not too busy."

"Come into my office." Mr. Jarves led the way into a carpeted room with a broad desk. "I'm looking for a man to rebuild and operate the pressing machine," he said.

For one wild moment Ben thought that he was being offered the job.

"I'm sure I could—" he began, but Mr. Jarves interrupted.

"What about Ira Benson? He wrote to me last fall, quite upset apparently that the glassworkers' children might starve, or some such nonsense. Do you think he might take the job?"

At first Ben could not find his voice. Hiding his disappointment, he choked, "He might, if you convinced him that the men no longer object to the machine."

Mr. Jarves had persuaded Pa to carry glassworks cargo on the *Orion*. Possibly he could sway Ira, too.

The next minute Mr. Jarves leaned forward and set his elbows on the desk. "I want you to know how very sorry I am about your father. I learned about the loss of his ship when I signed the insurance claims for the cargo during my stay in Boston."

"It doesn't seem right that he should have gone down with his ship," Ben said. For the life of him, he couldn't keep a tremor from his voice.

"I was deeply grieved to hear it." There was genuine concern in Deming Jarves's voice.

The bell on the rooftop clanged. A good thing, too. In another minute Ben would have told Mr. Jarves all the Tate family's troubles.

On the way home Ben reasoned with himself, struggling with his disappointment. Why should he have thought Mr. Jarves was offering him work on the pressing machine? He was just a newcomer and untried. Of

course, Ira, the original builder, should be the one to
operate and maintain successive models.

When he was halfway home, Ben realized that he had
not mentioned Karl Gantz's formula to Mr. Jarves. He
was certain now that it was a formula, although he realized that he must learn far more German before he
could understand it.

The next day Ben went again to the office.

The grim-faced clerk said shortly, "Mr. Jarves isn't
in. Do you want to leave a message?"

"It's about a formula for making glass," said Ben. "It
came from Germany, and it is very valuable."

The clerk threw back his head and laughed. "Not another one! If I had a dollar for every formula that's been
offered to the factory, I'd be a rich man. There was even
a foreign feller here one day, couldn't speak a word of
English, waving a formula in front of me. I sent him on
his way in a hurry."

"I'd like to talk to Mr. Jarves," Ben persisted.

"You'd be wasting your time," said the clerk. "Mr.
Jarves has spent years collecting formulas. There's nothing he doesn't know about glassmaking." He bent over
his ledger.

Ben left, slamming the door with satisfaction. He supposed he might as well give up. But some stubborn
streak in him refused to quit. Mr. Jarves himself had admitted there were mysteries about glass he hadn't yet
solved. Besides, the formula was Karl Gantz's gift to
Ben, and he would not be satisfied until he understood
it.

That afternoon a factory hand delivered a barrel of

flour to the Tate house. From his room above the kitchen Ben could hear his mother's puzzled voice.

"There must be some mistake," she said. "I didn't buy any flour."

"Mr. Jarves's orders, ma'am," the man said, and departed.

Grandfather stamped around. "Don't open the barrel," he cautioned. "Then you won't have to pay for it when the man takes it back."

Phoebe, when she came in from school, burst into tears. "Mr. Jarves sends a barrel of flour each year to the widows of glassworkers," she sobbed. "It's awful to have Pa dead, and to have to take charity."

"Charity or not, we can use it," said Ma in a tight voice.

In his chilly room, listening to every word, Ben grew so hot with anger that he had to take off his jacket. A barrel of flour! Fine compensation for a man's life. He walked up and down, clenching his fists.

The next pay day he went to the factory store and waited until all other customers had left. Mr. Griswold looked up at him expectantly, a smile on his thin face.

"A barrel of flour was delivered to my house," said Ben. "I want to pay for it."

Mr. Griswold brought out an account book. "My records show that barrel of flour was billed to Mr. Jarves's account."

Ben set his jaw. "I still want to pay for it," he said, and set the money on the counter.

Mr. Griswold turned his mild brown eyes on Ben. "You really mean it, don't you? Very well, I'll mark it paid by you, and credit Jarves's account with that amount." He scratched with his pen in the book, then closed it, adding, "I can understand how you feel, Ben. On the other hand, try to put yourself in Jarves's shoes. He was only trying to help."

"I don't need any help," said Ben.

"We all need help from one another," said Mr. Griswold. "Your trouble is that you always want to be the giver. You'll have to learn that accepting help is sometimes more difficult than giving it."

Perhaps Mr. Griswold is right, Ben thought as he headed home. For the first time he realized how difficult it must be for Ma to accept money from him. That must be why she was doing dressmaking. Poor Ma had certainly had a bad time, first losing Pa, and then being disappointed in her only son. He wished he could talk with her and explain how he felt. This afternoon he would try.

In the hours between dinner and supper three women came to the house for fittings. Ben studied with one ear cocked to the voices downstairs. When he heard Phoebe's treble, he lay down for a nap. His chance for a talk alone with Ma was gone for today.

Ben was not completely surprised, a few days later, to find Ira working at the pressing machine in the factory. Mr. Jarves was certainly a wizard at bending men to his will. The other workmen seemed undismayed. If they recognized the carpenter as the one-time target of their wrath, they kept the knowledge to themselves. Soon Ben had difficulty recalling what the factory had been like before Ira had come, his presence seemed so natural.

Summer came with its balmy breezes and fragrances
of locust and honeysuckle mingled with the tang of salt.
There were the gardens to cultivate alone, now that
Grandfather was too feeble to work. No matter how
hard Ben tried, he could not keep the weeds down. He
had not the time or strength to work at the factory and
keep the farm running normally. Give up his study of
German he would not. The hour with Emily was the
one bright spot in his day, and the slow, painful translation of the formula his secret hope for success.

Late in June Ben invited Emily to go with him to the
Fourth of July fireworks. On the afternoon of the great
day he called for her, scrubbed and as spruce as possible
in his old suit. Emily came to the door with a picnic
basket in her hand.

"Aunt Cassie is afraid that there will be too many
mosquitoes, so she's going to stay home," announced
Emily, her eyes dancing. "Papa says his idea of a perfect
holiday is not having to greet a single customer, so he's
going to stay home, too."

How anyone could elect to miss a Fourth of July cele-
bration, Ben did not know. But he was thankful to have
Emily to himself.

Emily smoothed her rose-and-white striped dress. "Do
you like it, Ben? It's my first new one in a year."

"It's fine," he said. Actually he had not realized her
dress was new. He thought Emily looked wonderful in
anything she wore.

As they neared the picnic grounds on the shore of the
millpond Emily and Ben became part of a crowd of people who moved about or sat under the trees, chatting,

laughing, and enjoying themselves. Some were dipping into picnic baskets. Others were ranged at long tables, eating delicacies prepared by ladies of the church.

Emily chose a quiet spot near the water for their supper. While she spread a cloth on the grass Ben went to a stand and bought two glasses of lemonade. Then he and Emily feasted and tossed bits of crust to the ducks on the pond. Chicken sandwiches and cherry cake had never tasted better to him.

Later they strolled around the grove while eleven young men tooted and trebled on three trombones, two bugles, five clarinets, and one trumpet, and a twelfth thumped on a bass drum. Though Emily winced now and then, claiming that the trumpet was out of tune, Ben thought he had never heard anything more beautiful. He could understand now why folks called music uplifting. He felt as if he could float right up in the air.

When the sun had set behind the ridge and darkness had set in, the fireworks began. First there were pin wheels and sparklers. Then came fancy set pieces, twinkling with hundreds of little flames, hissing like a thousand geese. And at the last, there were rockets, shooting showers of sparks, red, green, gold, and blue, above the still waters of the pond while the crowd sighed and gasped in wonder.

A final boom signaled the end of the display. Could it be over so soon? Ben stood up and reached down in the dark to help Emily to her feet. As she rose she stumbled and fell against him, her head on his shoulder. He held his breath, wishing she would never move. Then she straightened up, and the moment ended.

One day in August Ben asked Emily if he might borrow her German dictionary. When she hesitated, saying that she needed it for her own studies, he explained, "There's a paper written in German that I want to translate."

"If you bring it here, I'll help you with it," she offered.

Ben paused, undecided. Did he want to share his secret?

"I didn't mean to pry," Emily said, coloring. "Maybe it's something personal."

"Of course it's not personal," Ben said hastily. "But it is secret. You mustn't mention it to anyone."

Emily's eyes grew large with excitement. Ben hadn't noticed before how brown they were, and full of little lights.

"I won't say a word," she whispered.

When he spread the paper out before her the next day, she was at first mystified. "It's directions for making something," she said. "Did you ever hear of a glass called golden ruby?"

Ben's heart skipped a beat. Golden ruby! That was the glass Deming Jarves had spoken of when they were sailing from Sandwich to Boston. He could hear his voice now. "There's one colored glass I'd give anything to make—the golden ruby. Now only the Bohemians have the secret of its ingredients."

Suddenly a plan leaped into Ben's mind. He'd make the golden-ruby glass himself! Once the formula was translated, he could go ahead. In his present work he had access to ingredients and equipment for making glass. Deming Jarves would sit up and take notice when he saw that a newcomer to his factory had discovered the secret of golden-ruby glass. He would surely be rewarded.

Ben's voice was hoarse as he said, "Can you read any more?"

Emily frowned. "At the bottom it says, 'A special property of ruby glass is that—' That's all I can read. The next line is all blurred."

"That's where it got wet," said Ben. "Can you make out anything else?"

"There are lots of words I never saw before. They must be the ingredients. Let me see if they're in my dictionary." Emily riffled the pages, peered at the print, then looked back at the formula, and tried another word. Again and again she searched. Finally she said, "I'm afraid my dictionary doesn't cover those terms."

"Is there one at the Academy that does?" Ben asked. Now that he knew definitely that the formula was for making golden-ruby glass, he could hardly contain his impatience.

To his disappointment, Emily reported the next day that the only other German dictionary at the Academy contained no chemical terms. Her teacher said that there was one at Harvard College, and if her friend really needed the information, he should go to the library there.

All the way to Cambridge to look up some words? Ridiculous! Ben couldn't take time off from work, for one thing. Besides, a trip to Cambridge cost money, and he hadn't any cash to spare. Moreover, Harvard College was a place for professors and rich students. They probably wouldn't let a mere glassworker step inside the door.

But the more Ben pondered, the more clearly he realized that if he were to make ruby glass, he must go to Cambridge. For days he thought, and hourly his course grew more plain.

On Friday the glasshouse was shut down. Only the tiseurs were kept at work feeding long sticks of wood into the furnace, and a handful of men filling pots. Ben was usually among those, but someone else could take his place.

Instead of leaving all his pay on the clock shelf, Ben laid two dollars there and told Ma he needed the rest for a trip to Cambridge.

"It's your money, and you have the right to spend it as you wish," she said. "I think a change will do you good."

Phoebe gazed at him enviously. "I wish I could go with you."

"Not this time," Ben said gruffly. Secretly he vowed that when he could afford it, he would take Phoebe on a trip—Phoebe and Ma, too. But first he must translate the formula.

Friday morning Ben took the packet *Polly* to Boston. The day was fair, the sea calm, and the wind gentle. If he had not been so excited and impatient, Ben would have enjoyed the trip. Instead, he paced the deck almost continually, as if by his action he could speed the vessel more rapidly to its destination.

After a cheap dinner in a tavern, Ben walked around

the Boston docks, hoping to find the *Patent,* but the steamboat was evidently at her Maine port. Feeling lonely and strange, Ben returned to the *Polly* for the night, where Captain Fisher frequently let Sandwich folk sleep, so long as they were sober and not likely to set the vessel afire with their cigars.

Early Saturday morning Ben started for Cambridge. No coaches were running so early, so he followed the road signs, crossed the Charles River by the West Boston Bridge, and went along Main Street to Harvard Square. In a tavern still reeking with smoke and liquor from the night before, he had coffee, bread, and cheese. He asked the proprietor the way to the college library.

The man jerked his thumb toward a group of buildings around an open field. "There's Harvard College. Which hall is the library, I couldn't tell you. Chapel will be over in a minute or two. Why don't you ask one of the boys then?"

Ben crossed the dusty road and walked toward a small brick building from which issued the sound of young voices lifted in a hymn. Suddenly the door burst open and out trooped dozens of young men in black gowns. Before Ben could ask his question, they had hurried past.

A grave older man, also wearing a gown, followed the students. Ben stepped up to him.

"Can you please tell me the way to the library?"

The man looked up in mild surprise. "It's right there —in Harvard Hall. Just go up to the second floor. Mr. Pierce will take care of you."

Feeling very strange, Ben climbed the stairs to the library, where shelves of books were crowded into every inch of space. Mr. Pierce must be the young man standing by a window, engrossed in a thin volume.

"Do you have a German-English dictionary that contains chemical terms?"

"I think so." The man walked to a table, lifted a bulky volume, and handed it to Ben. "This should help you."

Trembling with excitement, Ben took out the list of ingredients that Emily had copied off for him. The sight of her neat handwriting was reassuring. Now, what was that first word? He turned the pages of the dictionary and began copying down the terms, feeling a strange elation as he found "sand," "red lead," and "potash."

While he worked the man who had directed him to the library came in and sat down at the table with him. The young man rose and asked, "Is there anything I can get for you, Professor Ferrar?"

"No, thank you," said the professor.

Ben looked up. To his knowledge, he'd never talked with a professor before. This man was as pleasant and modest appearing as any farmer in Sandwich, for all he was so learned.

"Have you found what you came after?" asked Professor Ferrar.

"I've found the names of the chemicals I wanted," said Ben. "Now I'll have to find out what these measurements are. Evidently Germans have a different system."

"Maybe I could help you," the man offered. "Those things are in my line."

"I'm used to dealing in ounces and pounds," said

Ben. "This is all in something called grams and kilograms."

"That's the metric system," said Professor Ferrar, "the only intelligent means of measurement. The Europeans are ahead of us, but we'll follow them in a year or two—just wait. All you have to do is remember that one ounce equals 28.35 grams, and one pound, .4536 kilograms. Here, I'll write it out for you." He put down the figures.

Until early afternoon Ben struggled with grams and ounces, kilograms and pounds. He dared not stop for lunch until he had finished his self-appointed task. When at last he had lists of quantities and ingredients with which he could make up a batch of mix for golden-ruby glass, he was exhausted but in high spirits.

Back in Boston, Ben found a fishing boat from Sandwich tied up at the wharf. Yes, they would sail back home tomorrow, Sabbath or no. Ben was welcome to go with them if he'd watch the vessel during the evening while the crew sought some entertainment.

Ben spent the evening going over his figures. The crew came back very late and very drunk. Sunday was stormy and rainy, and Ben was sick all the way down Massachusetts Bay. He didn't really care. He had accomplished what he intended—making the formula workable.

Glass Fever

Monday morning Ben thought he could not possibly summon the strength to go to work. But the sheet with the scribbled list of ingredients and the amounts of each gave him the impetus he needed. He got through the morning hours, slept most of the afternoon, and arrived at Emily's house at a quarter before six.

"Could you find the words?" she asked as she opened the door.

"Yes, and the weights, too." He told about his meeting with Professor Ferrar.

"Let's write it out, then," she said, her eagerness matching his.

Together they sat at the sitting-room table, bent over the worn sheet of paper. Emily wrote in English the ingredients as Ben read them off, one by one, consulting first Karl Gantz's neat script, then his own notes.

When he had finished, Emily said, "There's one more ingredient—one ounce of gold. I found that in my dictionary, so I didn't put it on the list."

"An ounce of gold!" Ben was dumfounded. "Where

can I get an ounce of gold? Do you realize that's what's in a twenty-dollar gold piece?"

"You could save up for it," Emily said.

"On five dollars and fifty cents a week?" Ben said. "And the family needing every penny?" He felt as if the world had suddenly turned topsy-turvy. "I might as well give up. It was just a foolish idea."

Emily stood up, her eyes blazing. "It is not a foolish idea!" she cried, stamping her foot. "You've worked so hard on this, you can't give up now. You'll have to get the gold somehow."

"What do you want me to do—steal it?" Ben asked grimly.

"Don't be silly," she said. "Doesn't someone in your family have gold jewelry? Aunt Cassie has two brooches and her husband's cuff links and watch chain."

Ben shook his head slowly. "Pa had a gold watch, but he always carried it with him. Ma hasn't any jewelry. I don't think there's a bit of gold in our house—except Ma's wedding ring."

They were both silent.

"I could ask Aunt Cassie for the cuff links," Emily offered.

Now it was Ben's turn to shoot sparks. "Don't you dare!" he said hotly. "I'd rather wait until I can save the money—even a few cents a week."

"You'll be an old man by the time you save enough," Emily said.

Ben was about to answer angrily when the factory bell rang. He picked up the papers, stuffed them into his pocket, and stalked out of the house. For the first time Emily did not accompany him to the door.

Somehow Ben got through the evening, each hour dragging. When he came out into the cool night, the moonlight and fragrant air seemed at variance with his mood. By rights a storm should be raging.

When he reached home, he found the door ajar and a shadowy form on one of the porch chairs.

"Who's there?" he asked cautiously.

Ma's voice answered. "It's such a lovely night I thought I'd sit out here for a while. It's better than lying in bed awake and worrying."

Ben sat on the steps and let his head rest on his knees. "I wish you wouldn't worry, Ma."

"How can I help it? It may have been God's will that I should lose your father. But it's my own selfish fault that I've lost my son." Her voice broke.

Ben could feel tears trickling onto his hands. "You haven't lost me, Ma," he said. "I'm right here."

"You might as well be a thousand miles away," she said, "for all the good we are to each other. We never talk any more. We could be strangers."

"I can't help it if I don't want to be a doctor. I know I'm a disappointment to you." All his pent up misery surged through him.

"I'm not disappointed in you. I'm proud of you," said Ma. "Nobody works any harder than you—and you're studying, too."

Ben felt choked. "The studying is all over," he said morosely.

"But you seemed so interested!"

"Not any more. I know when I'm licked." In a low voice he told her about the paper Karl Gantz had given him, how he had struggled to discover its meaning, and having succeeded, had come up against a final, insurmountable obstacle.

"You can get all the other things you need?" Ma asked.

"Yes, except for a few ounces of chemicals which cost only a few cents, they are all at the glassworks. I handle them every day, and I'm sure Mr. Frisbee would let me have the small quantities I'd need."

"If you had some gold, you could go ahead?" Ma asked.

"That's right," he said. Why did she have to repeat what was so obvious, and so painful?

In the moonlight Ben could see that Ma was pulling at her finger. She leaned toward him and held out her hand. "Here, Son, do you think this will be enough?"

The ring was still warm. He held it for a moment, tempted beyond reason. Then he dropped it in her lap.

"I couldn't take your wedding ring, Ma. It's all you have left."

"What nonsense! I have you and Honor and Phoebe, and my memories. That's more than lots of women ever have. The ring is mine to do with as I please. I can invest it any way I want, and I choose to put it into your future." She was laughing shakily.

He must be dreaming. Everything seemed unreal. "You'll regret it in the morning, Ma."

"No, I won't. I've never been more sure of anything in my life. You take it, Ben, with my blessing."

The next morning Ben woke to sunlight glinting on the ring as it lay on his bureau. It was real, and so was his chance to try out the formula. With a bound he was out of bed.

After the morning's work Ben stopped at the shop of the town's goldsmith, who was also a silversmith and maker of false teeth.

"Can you tell me how much a wedding ring weighs?" he asked.

The man peered through brass-rimmed glasses. "You thinking of getting married?" he asked. "That Griswold girl seems right smart."

Ben swallowed. A vision flashed into his mind of Emily greeting him at the door every evening. The prospect was dazzling. Then he remembered their heated parting yesterday.

"I just want to know how much this ring weighs," he said, drawing the gold circlet from his pocket.

The man took the heavy ring, set it on a small scale in back of the counter, and poked delicately at a tiny weight on the balance bar.

"That's eleven pennyweights," he said judiciously.

Nothing about pennyweights had come up in the discussion at the Harvard Library.

"How much is that?" Ben asked.

"Just a touch over half an ounce," said the man.

"Of pure gold?" asked Ben.

"Not quite. You have to figure that about one quarter is base metal—copper in this ring, I'd say." He squinted at it.

"Then there's less than half an ounce. How much would you think?"

"About three-eighths of an ounce. Say, what do you want to know this for? You planning to sell it?"

"Not on your life," said Ben. "I'm going to use it."

"I knew you were interested in that girl," cackled the man.

Ben didn't bother to answer. Besides, he could not honestly say he was not interested in Emily.

Next he must buy the chemicals for preparing the gold. He leaned against an elm tree and consulted the directions anew, wondering how he could have over-looked earlier the word *Gold*. Any fool would recognize it for "gold."

If the ring weighed three-eights of an ounce, he'd need that fraction of the other ingredients. With a pen-cil he calculated on a scrap of paper, then entered the chemist's shop. The man stared when he ordered one ounce of sal ammoniac acid, five and a half ounces of nitric acid, one ounce of muriatic acid, and a half ounce of alcohol.

"Have you decided to go in with Doc Dow after all?" he asked.

"No," Ben said shortly. In Sandwich a person couldn't turn around without the whole town knowing about it.

With chemicals, ring, and formula, he jogged home. Ma had kept dinner waiting, but better than the hot meal was her smile. It warmed him clear down to his toes.

Although he knew that the changing of the gold into

the purple of Cassius would take nine days, Ben had not imagined how impatient he would become during that period. While he restlessly endured the passage of time he fought for patience. He had struggled for almost a year to unlock Karl Gantz's secret. Surely he could wait a few days longer to ensure success in making the sought-after glass. If he could have talked with Emily, the time would have passed more quickly. But he could not bring himself to ask her pardon. Before he cut the ring into ten tiny fragments as directed, Ben held it toward Ma and asked gently, "Do you want to change your mind?"

The smile she gave him was firm. "Certainly not."

Six days for the sal ammoniac and nitric acids to merge, and another day for the pieces of the gold ring to dissolve. Then the solution must be evaporated to leave a precipitate.

Twenty-four hours for the prepared gold mixed with nitric and muriatic acids and alcohol, plus eighty times as much water, to settle. Another twenty-four hour wait while the settlings were mixed with eleven ounces of water, allowed to stand, and strained.

The powdery residue Ben wrapped tenderly in a sheet of Ma's best note paper before supper one evening. "I'll stay after work and mix it," he said, tucking the small square deep in his pocket with the formula.

During a lull in the night's work, Ben went to the pot room. Although he had been there many times before, he was shaking with excitement.

"I'd like a monkey pot, please," he said, wondering if his voice betrayed his feeling.

"How about this one?"

"Thanks." Ben placed it in the furnace to heat on top of one of the gigantic pots.

At midnight he said to Mr. Frisbee, trying not to sound as self-conscious as he felt, "I'm going to stay to mix up a special batch."

"I was wondering how soon you'd catch the glass fever," said Dan. "Good luck to you." He thumped Ben on the shoulder as he left.

The Experiment

Ben measured out the required quantities—twelve pounds of silex, nine and three-quarter pounds of red lead, six pounds of nitre, and so on. At the very last he added the powdered gold. When they were mingled to his satisfaction, he wheeled them to the furnace, filled the monkey pot, and covered it. As he walked away he realized that his knees were shaking.

Now he had nothing to do but wait. A regular batch of glass required about forty-eight hours to melt. The small pot took a shorter time, twelve hours or so. Perhaps by tomorrow noon his batch would be ready.

He was so keyed up he could hardly sleep. To Ma's unspoken question at breakfast, he said, "It's melting now. We'll know by this afternoon."

She gave him a steady smile, and he hurried off to the factory. Near the Griswold house his steps slowed. Emily would not have left for the Academy yet. Perhaps he should stop in and tell her that the glass was melting. But the memory of their quarrel was still vivid, and he continued on.

When he wheeled a truck of flint-glass mix toward the furnace, he peered into the monkey pot. The contents had liquefied and were filled with bubbles. They would cook out, he knew from experience. If only the glass would be ready to work by noon.

Martin came up and plunged his rod into the next pot. "You cooking up a batch, Ben?"

"That's right," said Ben.

"It looks different," said Martin.

"It ought to."

"Going to try it out this noon?" asked Martin.

Ben nodded.

"I could stick around if you want," offered Martin.

"Thanks, but I can manage all right," said Ben. When he put the golden-ruby glass into the press, he didn't want any help. The triumph was to be his, and his alone. He had watched the men poke their long iron rods into the melt, twist them around, and pull out gobs of glass. It looked easy enough.

Noontime came. In the glasshouse only the boys remained, clearing up after the last move. Ben had an hour before the next shift came on.

Six pressing machines stood along one wall, Salt dishes, cup plates, and inkwells were turned out of their molds in large quantities during the day. Ben chose the inkwell press. He could see a glowing ruby inkwell on the center of a teacher's desk, and Emily saying to a classroom of attentive pupils, "It was given to me by a dear friend. He's a famous glassmaker now."

Hardly breathing for excitement, Ben approached the small pot. The glass in it was smooth and glossy, and red with heat. He picked up an iron rod and dipped it into the liquid, twirling it as he had seen glassmakers do.

When he lifted the rod, the liquid fell from it. He must have been too hasty. He tried again, using the motions he had observed hundreds of time. Once more the molten glass slid back into the pot. Furious, Ben took a firmer grip on the rod. After all his pains, would he be unable to move the glass from pot to press?

He was ready to give up when a mocking voice at his elbow said, "Sure, and you can manage all right."

Ben whirled, almost knocking the pot over. "Where did you come from?"

"I forgot my coat," said Martin. "You want me to give it a try?" He cocked an eye at Ben.

Gratefully Ben handed over the rod.

In a few seconds Martin had worked up a gather on the rod by dipping up a small portion of glass, letting it cool, then adding more, and was rushing it to the pressing machine. Ben followed, and as the gob of glass landed in the mold he pushed with all his strength on the lever. A minute later he raised it, then opened the mold, plucked out the inkwell, and set it on a tray.

Ben peered at it anxiously, wishing the glasshouse was better lighted. The shadows here were deep.

"It doesn't look like much," he said to Martin.

"You can't tell anything about glass until it comes out of the lehr," Martin said, looking toward the big annealing oven where the finished pieces were kept in gradually decreasing temperatures until cool.

"I'm not going to bother with the lehr," said Ben. He could not stand any further suspense.

"It's your batch," said Martin. "You've still got a lot left in the monkey. Want to use it up?"

"You don't mind staying?"

"I'm here, ain't I? Let's get busy."

Together the two worked swiftly, Martin filling the

mold and Ben pushing down on the lever and removing
the inkwells. He had to hurry to keep up with Martin.
He was so excited that his hands were wet with perspira-
tion. Would the glass have the golden glow that was the
mark of the true ruby? He could hardly wait to finish
and take a piece into the light.

When Martin had emptied the monkey pot and Ben
had given the lever a last thrust, he straightened up,
shaking with anticipation. Now, at last, he would see the
fabulous golden-ruby glass.

He carried the tray of inkwells to the open door of the
furnace and examined them in the brilliant light. For a
moment he could not believe his eyes. There they stood,
a full two dozen, and every one the ugliest, dirtiest
yellow-gray he had ever seen. He was about to dash
them to the floor when Martin joined him.

"They didn't turn out as you hoped?" he asked.

Ben set his jaw so fiercely that his teeth ground together. "No," he said. The tray in his hands was shaking, the inkwells rattling against one another.

"That happens a good many times," said Martin.
"You need a lot of patience in this business. Maybe next
time you'll have better luck."

"There'll never be a next time," Ben stormed. How
could there be, when he had used all the gold in Ma's
ring in this batch? He half threw the tray on the floor in
a dark corner and started away. The sooner he got out
of this place, the better. At the last minute, he stooped,
picked up one of the small gray inkwells, and slipped it
into his pocket.

As Ben walked along Dock Lane the clock in the
church tower struck one. Emily would be home for din-

ner. He might as well stop at her house. He owed her an explanation, at least.

Emily, answering the door, was stiffly polite. "Good afternoon, Mr. Tate," she said coolly. "Would you care to come in?"

"Just for a minute, Miss Griswold," Ben said, following her into the sitting room. The room looked so cosy, with a fire crackling in the fireplace to ward off the chill, that he wished he could sit down. Emily's ramrod stance prevented him.

"I wanted to report to you about the formula," said Ben. "My mother gave me her wedding ring, and I was able to make the experiment. But it was a complete failure." He drew out the inkwell and held it on the palm of his hand. "See?"

Horrified, Emily looked at it. "Oh, Ben," she cried, her own self once more, "Something must have gone wrong."

"Very wrong," he said. "I followed the instructions to the letter, but the glass didn't turn out right. Karl Gantz tricked me into believing that formula was worth something. He was just a cheat." Suddenly Ben realized that he was as upset about his disappointment in Karl Gantz as about the failure of the formula.

"Oh, Ben, don't talk like that. You really liked him. I can't believe he meant to deceive you." Emily was close to tears.

"Well, he did. And I'm through. I never want to see another piece of glass." With one swift movement Ben hurled the inkwell into the fire. It sent up a shower of sparks and disappeared behind a flaming log.

"And I never want to look at the formula again, either," Ben said. He drew the papers from his pocket, crumpled them into a ball, and threw them after the inkwell. They exploded in flame, and in a minute were gone.

"That's the end of that." Ben turned on his heel.

"What are you going to do?" quavered Emily.

"I don't know," said Ben. "I'd like to get as far away as I can from Sandwich and the glassworks. Maybe I'll go to Boston." He had reached the door when honesty prevailed. "That's what I'd like to do. But I'll have to stay here and keep on working at the factory."

"Can't your mother and sister look out for themselves?" Emily asked. "It's terrible for you to work at something you hate."

"No, they can't," said Ben. "They need a man to look after them, and Grandfather's too old." He stalked away, so filled with anger and discouragement that he could have howled like a dog in his frustration.

At home, all seemed serene. Phoebe was arranging bittersweet in a copper bowl. Ma was peeling potatoes, and a rich aroma of roasting meat pervaded the kitchen.

"The butcher's wife paid me for her dress with a piece of beef," Ma said happily. "It's just in time to celebrate your—" She broke off as she looked at Ben's face. "Did something go wrong, Son? Didn't the glass turn out as you expected?"

"No, it didn't," he said, and stamped upstairs. He couldn't look at Ma any longer. Her bare third finger was in itself a reproach. And if she gave him any sympathy, he'd break down. That was the last thing he wanted to do. All he had left was his self-control, and that was slipping fast.

In his bedroom he lay down, not bothering to take off his shoes. He'd have to do some thinking, that was sure. Any hopes he'd had of making a fortune by selling the formula to Mr. Jarves had gone up in smoke. He'd just have to stay in Sandwich and keep on working. Dr. Dow had been right in his prediction. Ben would probably spend the rest of his life shoveling sand.

Angrily he thumped his pillow. If he were free, he'd go to Boston and get that job on the steamboat. There were probably lots of jobs in Boston a hundred times more interesting than his work as a filler. If only he weren't saddled with a family to support.

The roast beef was so tough it slithered across his plate when he tried to cut it. Phoebe struggled wordlessly with hers, but Ma said cheerfully, "It's tasty enough. I'll make it into stew tomorrow."

Tomorrow. Ben didn't know how he could live through another day. Like an automaton he went to work and came home, went to bed, and returned to the factory. For the rest of his days he'd be doing the same, he figured. The future stretched ahead drearily.

At home the next afternoon he went to his room and lay down. There were plenty of chores, but he could find neither the energy nor the spirit to do them. Let Phoebe take care of the animals. It wouldn't hurt her. Let Grandfather bring in the pumpkins. He still had a little strength left. Even when Ben heard the voices of Honor and Caleb, and Noah's prattle, he remained upstairs. He was in no mood to face anyone.

At Ma's call he came down for supper. She had persuaded Honor and Caleb to stay and was ladling out the stew, rich with chunks of beef. Honor was tying a bib on

Noah, and Caleb was setting a billet of wood on a chair for the baby to sit on. Grandfather waited at his place, drumming with corded fingers on the table. Beside the window, Phoebe peered out into the dusk.

"There's a man in the road," she said.

"Is he coming in here?" asked Ma.

"No," said Phoebe. "He's gone past our walk." She waited a minute, then said, "He's turned around and is coming back."

"He probably forgot something," said Ma. "Take this bowl to Grandfather, please."

Phoebe set the steaming dish on the table, then stood by the window once more. "He's coming back again, Mamma. The way he's walking gives me the queerest feeling."

Ben joined her at the window. "What's so queer about him?"

"He acts like Pa!" said Phoebe, her voice taut.

Ma dropped the ladle into the kettle so abruptly that some of the contents spilled out upon the iron lids and began to hiss and burn. She paid it no heed. Her hand flew to her throat. She took one look out the window, dashed out the door, quick as a flash, and started running.

"Phoebe, you shouldn't have said that," said Ben.

His sister wasn't listening. She gave a shriek and followed Ma down the path, skimming over the ground like a bird.

Ben stood in the doorway, unable to believe his eyes. There in the road stood a man, one arm around Ma, the other reaching out for Phoebe. There was no doubt about it. Pa *had* come home!

Freedom

And what a confused homecoming it was, with the family rejoicing and weeping and laughing all at once out in the roadway! Somehow after a time they made their way into the house. Somehow they all sat around the table and ate supper, although no one knew whether the dishes contained stew or ambrosia.

When they were settled in the sitting room, with some semblance of normality, Phoebe demanded, "Why weren't you drowned, Pa?"

Trust Phoebe to ask Pa such a question, thought Ben.

Ma was sitting on the sofa beside Pa, clinging to his arm as if she would never let go. "I knew you were alive somewhere," she said, her face aglow. Ben flinched at the memory of the times he had doubted her. "There must have been some good reason why you didn't write," continued Ma.

"At first I hadn't the strength," said the captain, "and then, God forgive me, I doubted whether I'd reach home at all. I thought it would be harder for you to get a letter saying I was alive, and later learn that I'd been drowned trying to get here." He stroked Ma's hand. "I was thinking of you all the time, Margaret. I hope what I did was right."

Ma smiled and nodded, too choked up to say more.

"How did you get off the *Orion*, Pa?" Ben asked. "The hardest thing I ever did was to row away and leave you."

"For me, too," said Caleb fervently. He had hardly taken his eyes off Pa.

"There wasn't anything else you could do," said Pa. "And things worked out all right. I'm here, you see."

Ben saw the same sturdy, sunburned man who had left Sandwich a year before. His hair was more streaked with gray, though, and his eyes had a look of suffering that was past but not forgotten. "How *did* you get off, Pa?" demanded Ben. "I know the *Orion* sank. I saw her starting to break up."

His father's eyes darkened. "At dusk, just as I had given up hope, the brig *Peacock* came along and took me aboard. In a few hours we ran into another storm, and she lost her masts. We finally put into Antigua under jury rig, but by that time I was very sick, and they left me there. It took me weeks to recover; after that I had to wait for passage home. I managed to get a ship to Charleston, then one to Philadelphia, and another to Boston. And here I am."

"Oh, Cyrus, I do thank God for your deliverance," Ma whispered. "I can't tell you how it grieves me, though, to think of your being sick so far away from home."

Into Ben's mind flashed a picture of the stranger Ma

had nursed during Pa's absence. Had that been just coincidence, or was it part of some vast plan?

Captain Tate took Noah on his knee and dandled him happily.

"Why did you walk up and down in front of the house so many times, Papa?" asked Phoebe. "Were you afraid to come in?"

"I feared that if I came right up to the door, the shock would be too much for your mother," he said. "You remember Etta Beasley."

For a minute they were all silent. Captain Beasley, like Pa, had been thought drowned and had returned after a long absence. When his wife opened the door and saw him, she suffered a heart attack and died within minutes.

The captain looked around at his family. "I still can't believe I'm here," he said. "We had a fierce storm between Charleston and Philadelphia. I truly thought my end had come."

Ben listened incredulously. Pa had never before expressed any doubt as to his safety at sea. He'd always been full of confidence.

Pa turned to Grandfather, who was sitting like a statue, his faded eyes brimming.

"You were right when you said that one day I'd be glad to turn my hand to farming. From now on I mean to abide on dry land, our own land, here in Sandwich."

Ben could hardly believe his ears. "You mean you're going to stay here and farm?"

"Unless you and Father think I'll be in your way."

In their way! Grandfather was hardly strong enough

to hold a rake. And Ben had merely scratched at the most neglected spots. Pa couldn't have paid much attention to the fields and gardens when he was walking up and down in front of the house.

"I thought Caleb might help me clear a few acres, and we could plant potatoes. It's nonsense for the factory store to bring them down from New Hampshire when we can grow them here. How about it, Caleb?"

"Oh, Pa, that would be wonderful!" said Honor, radiant.

"Suits me fine," said Caleb. Ben suspected that he had not enjoyed driving the bull wagons.

"I must say you all look well." Pa eyed each beaming face. "Thank heaven I took out insurance on the *Orion* before I left. It was the one thing that buoyed me up while I was sick. At least I hadn't left you without funds."

Ma and Ben exchanged glances. "Insurance?" they asked together.

Grandfather looked down. His hands trembled.

"Of course," said Pa. "I gave the policy to Father."

The old man's chin began to quiver. "I can't remember things the way I used to."

Ben couldn't help but feel sorry for him. At the same time he was furious. The insurance money would have made a world of difference to them all.

"You put it away. I saw you," said the captain to his father. He went to Grandfather's desk in the corner, let down its polished lid, and tugged at one of the small drawers. "Do you have the key, Father?" he asked patiently. "I think you put the policy in here."

Grandfather fumbled in his pocket and brought out a key ring. Cyrus unlocked the drawer and drew forth a document covered with fine print. He scanned it hastily.

"There doesn't seem to be any time limit on claims," he said, and put it down.

"To think it was there all the time, and I didn't know," said Ma. "You might have told me, Cyrus." Her tone was reproving.

"We men have always handled money matters," said Pa lamely. His tone changed to one of anxiety. "How did you manage? Did you have enough to eat? What about the taxes? Did you sell some land?"

Ma sat up straight and tall. "Our son has taken care of us while you were away. If it hadn't been for him, we might have gone hungry. He even earned enough to pay the taxes so we could keep the roof over our heads."

Ben met Pa's glance, and found in it a new respect.

"How did you earn the money?" asked the captain.

"At the glassworks," said Ben. "I'm a filler."

As he spoke the factory bell rang out. He sprang to his feet. Nearly seven o'clock already! If he ran all the way, taking short cuts, he might possibly get there in time.

When he reached the glasshouse door, Martin was waiting for him. "That was hard luck about your glass," he said sympathetically.

Ben had been so up in the clouds about Pa's return that he had almost forgotten the glass failure. Misery flooded over him anew. He made his way to the mixing room and his waiting truck.

So much had happened, Ben's mind was in a whirl. He hadn't yet thought out the full significance of Pa's return and the existence of the insurance policy. The money from the *Orion*'s insurance would amply provide for the family. Pa could afford to hire a man or two and farm on a large enough scale to make considerable profit. Most glassworkers had no gardens of their own and were willing to pay good prices for fresh vegetables and fruits.

Suddenly he realized that there was no longer any need for him to remain at the glass factory. He was free! Any day he could quit his job and go off wherever he wanted to do whatever he pleased. He could even go to Boston and work on the *Patent*. The prospect should have been exhilarating, but for some reason he couldn't get excited about it. Probably he was tired. Tomorrow he would feel more enthusiastic.

But the next day Ben was still unhappy and uncertain. On his way to work he thought, I'll give my notice today. Once that's done, I'll feel better.

At noontime, as Ben walked through the glasshouse, Ira called out to him.

"Take a look at this, will thee, Ben? Maybe thee can figure out how to avoid this thickness at the rim." He held out a tumbler with an uneven lip.

Ben looked at the plunger on the machine. "Could you put a flange on it that would fit over the top part of the mold? Something like an inverted pie plate?

"That might do it," Ira said. He scratched his head. "Has thee thought about working on the machines? I need another man, and I'd like well to have thee."

A week ago Ben would have jumped at the chance. Now he hesitated. "You've heard about my father coming home?" he asked.

"The whole town knows," said Ira. "Good news spreads as fast as bad. I can imagine how thankful thy family is."

"I still can't believe he's alive," said Ben. He pulled his thoughts back, and added, "Ma won't be needing my pay any more, so I think I'll give up my job and go to Boston to work on that steamboat."

"I recall that thee was much taken with the steam engine," said Ira. "But before thee decides, it might be well to give the matter some thought. There's no telling what we couldn't build here. Thy mind and mine work well together."

It was true. Where Ira's ideas left off, Ben's went on. And the other way around. Together they could work out almost anything.

Resolutely Ben turned away. He was through with glass. His experiment had been an abysmal failure. It was time for him to leave the factory and go on to something else. He headed for the office.

The door was locked, and there was no response to his knock. Then he saw the small sign in a corner of the glass. Back at two. The clerk must have gone to his dinner while Ben was talking with Ira. He turned away. Tomorrow would be time enough to give his notice.

Ben walked toward home, scuffing dry leaves underfoot. The October sky was a bright blue, and the sun brilliant, but he could feel no answering lift of the spirits. More than ever he was dismayed by the failure of Karl Gantz's formula. Once again he went over the process. Somewhere he had done something wrong—but what?

Passing the Griswold house, he looked at the windows for a glimpse of Emily. Each curtained pane was lifeless. Emily must be at the Academy. She was probably disgusted with him for taking so much of her time to give him German lessons only to have all her effort wasted. He kicked savagely at a stone in the road.

Nearing home, he could hear the blows of a hammer, and as he walked up the path he saw his father at the back steps, replacing a worn tread.

"Hello, Pa," he said. For the life of him he couldn't keep the despair out of his voice.

The captain stood up, gave him a keen glance, and said, "How about stopping for a minute? I haven't had a chance to talk with you since I got back. How is your job going?"

"All right, I guess," said Ben.

"Do you like working at the factory?"

"I did—that is—until—"

The captain eyed him keenly. "Has something gone wrong? At first I thought you had become serious because you had all the responsibility of the family while I was away. But now I suspect there's more of a reason."

"There is," said Ben miserably. "I didn't want to bother you just as you got home, but I guess you ought to know." He poured out the story of Karl Gantz and the formula, of Emily's teaching him German, his trip to Cambridge, and of his mixing the trial batch—and its failure.

Pa listened quietly. At the end he asked, "And what do you plan to do now?"

"Get away," said Ben. "I've made such a botch of

things around here that I think I ought to start out fresh
somewhere else."

The captain stared at the marsh. "And where do you
plan to go?"

Ben told him.

"Hmmm." Pa studied the hammer in his hand.
"What about all the people who made the experiment
possible? Karl Gantz, first of all. Then Emily, and the
professor at Harvard. It seems to me quite a few others
were involved, too—Dan Frisbee, your friend Martin,
and Mr. Jarves—"

"I didn't ask Mr. Jarves for help!" blurted Ben.

"You used his materials and his furnace, didn't you,
and his pressing machine?"

Ben was silent. Pa was right. Without the factory and
its equipment he could not have attempted the experiment.

"Just think how you would feel," said Pa, "if you had
given your time and materials and effort to help someone, and he gave up and walked off."

"I don't see what else I can do," Ben said. Couldn't
Pa understand what it was like to fail so miserably?

"You might give the matter some serious thought before you go rushing off," Pa said.

Ben rose and went into the house before he exploded
into anger. Didn't Pa realize that he'd been thinking of
nothing else but the formula? Besides, he was tired of
having people tell him to give matters some thought.
First Ira. Then Pa. Did they think he never used his
brain?

The Glass Phoenix

That afternoon Ben headed for the beach, clamming fork and basket in hand. He needed to think, and there was no better place than an empty stretch of shore with the steady, continuing roll of the surf.

Walking barefoot onto the flats, he could feel some of his misery dissipating in the fresh breeze. As soon as he dug the fork into the wet sand, his mind began to clear.

Until now, he saw, he'd not been really thinking at all —just brooding over the failure of the formula. He recalled Pa's words. He had a good point when he said Ben owed something to those who had helped him. That was probably why he hadn't been glad about going to Boston. The least he could do was explain to his friends that he was leaving—and why.

He could see himself talking with each one—Martin, Dan Frisbee, and Emily. He could hear his own voice, strangely unconvincing, and their response. They would be polite, he knew, but inwardly all three would think the same—that he was quitting.

Savagely he swung the clamming fork and threw a

clam into the basket with such force that the tender shell cracked. Well, what was wrong with quitting? Didn't a man have to decide for himself when it was time to make a change? In Boston he could learn about steamboats, and then—And then what? He might become a captain of a steamboat. But what kind of future was that? Actually it was little different from being the captain of a sailing ship. He had no desire to go to sea. What he was interested in was the engine, but on the ship all he could do was operate it—not make changes or improve models.

He had a knack with machinery, he knew. Again he heard Ira's words. "There's no telling what we couldn't build here. Thy mind and mine work well together."

If he remained at the factory, what would the future hold for him? Not the glory of discovering the secret of golden-ruby glass, or a great sum of money for finding it. But there would be steady work, and the chance to use his ingenuity and knowledge of mechanics.

He looked at the waves rippling shoreward in unending rhythm. Their motion went on night and day, eternally. A man needed something stable in his life, a continuing interest to occupy his mind and strength. Ben had enjoyed feeling that he was a part of the glassworks. Perhaps he had better not leave just yet. Tomorrow he would tell Ira that he would work with him on the pressing machines.

The decision gave him new energy. Speedily he uncovered more clams and filled his basket.

When he reached the factory that night, Ben couldn't help looking in the corner where he had thrown the inkwells. It was empty and swept clean. Without asking, he knew that they had been thrown into the cullet bin with other broken and discarded pieces to be ground and added to new batches of mix. He'd do well to clear his mind completely of all thoughts of the golden-ruby glass.

As Ben wheeled his truck toward the furnace he looked around with new eyes. What he had at first considered complete confusion, he saw now as an intricate pattern of skilled teamwork. Each gaffer directed operations with an authority he had earned by skill and hard work. Around him worked his helpers, handling their special tools with lightning speed and precision.

On the other side of the glasshouse ranged the pressing machines. Here again there was teamwork of a high caliber. As the gatherer dropped molten glass into the mold the man on the lever threw his weight upon it instantly.

While he shoveled the mix into the giant pot Ben remembered how he had first recoiled from the heat of the furnace. Now he was accustomed to it. He looked into the pot with a practiced eye. The melt was coming along well. This would be a good batch.

On the next furnace sat a monkey pot, and it reminded him of the failure of his experiment. For a moment Ben was almost sick with disappointment. Then he pulled himself together. There was more to glassmaking than finding new formulas.

Just as he started to wheel his empty truck toward the mixing room, a new boy rushed toward him, a glowing champagne glass on the end of his forked stick. Ben stepped back. The boy's foot struck a piece of cullet, and he started to fall toward the bubbling monkey pot. Automatically Ben reached out and caught the boy's arm, steadying him. The boy regained his balance and continued on toward the lehr, the glass miraculously still on the stick.

It was all over in a minute, and Ben continued on to the mixing room. Six months ago he would not have been familiar enough with the hazards of the glasshouse to save the boy from striking against the monkey pot and being seriously, perhaps fatally burned. Now it was all part of the night's work.

The next day Ben sought out Ira. "I'd like to take that job you offered," he said. "Of course, I'll have to give Dan Frisbee notice first."

"Thee has decided not to go to Boston?"

Ben nodded. "I'd rather stay here and work with you."

Ira's smile warmed Ben through and through.

At noontime Ben left the factory and started home. A block away he saw Dr. Dow's buggy pull up before a house. Ben was tempted to cross the street so that he would not have to speak. He had not seen the doctor since the day he had announced he didn't want to study medicine.

Dr. Dow must have had the same thought. He appeared to be examining the contents of his black bag.

It was the hardest task of Ben's life to keep on walking down the road. As he came abreast of the buggy he stopped and said, "Good morning, sir." The words almost stuck in his throat.

The doctor looked up. "Oh, hello, Ben."

Ben took a deep breath. "I just wanted to say— I meant to tell you that day, that I really appreciated your wanting to help me. It's just that I don't think I'm cut out to be a doctor. You must have thought I was interested because I wanted Narcissa's leg to heal. I was, but not as a doctor would be. I wanted to rig up something to keep her off the floor. You understand, don't you?"

"I think so," said Dr. Dow. "It's just as well you reached that conclusion before we had both put a lot of effort into your education." He closed his bag. "What are you doing now?"

"Working at the glass factory. I'll be helping Ira figure out new ways of pressing glass, and maybe other new machines."

"That's good," the doctor said. "I was afraid you might be shoveling sand the rest of your life, but I should have known better." He jumped out of the carriage. "I've got to go in here and set a broken leg—on a human patient." He grinned, and patted Ben's shoulder. "Good luck in your job."

Ben walked on, squaring his shoulders. He hadn't realized before how much he had minded the break with Dr. Dow. It was a good feeling to be friends with him once more. The sky seemed suddenly brighter.

Near Emily's house Ben slowed his steps. Some of the misery he had felt the last time he had seen her came back to him. He hoped that she didn't feel that all her tutoring had been in vain. At least he had learned enough German so that he could read it fairly well. He could even write the script, though slowly.

Emily had seemed terribly disappointed at the failure

of the formula. She might not have much use for him now that there was no chance of his discovering the golden-ruby glass.

He was passing the front steps when the door flew open, and Emily appeared, broom in hand. At the sight of Ben, she stopped short.

"What wonderful news about your father coming home! You must be very thankful."

"It's like a miracle. I can still hardly believe it," said Ben.

"Now you'll be able to go to Boston. Will you be leaving soon?"

Something in her tone made Ben look at her closely.

"I'm not going," he said. "I suppose it sounds dull and uninteresting to you, but I'm going to stay at the factory."

"I thought you hated your work," said Emily, frowning.

"Not truly," said Ben. "I was so disappointed about the formula that I hated everything about glass for a while. But that's all over now. I'm going to have a new job helping Ira Benson with the pressing machines."

"Like the one you helped him build at first? Oh, Ben, that's wonderful!" He'd never seen her smile so brightly.

"You don't mind that I didn't discover how to make ruby glass?"

"Of course not. I was just awfully sorry for you, after you had worked so hard on the formula. And I miss your coming every day for your lesson." She stopped suddenly and began sweeping the steps.

"This is a strange time of day for you to be sweeping," said Ben. "Why aren't you on your way back to the Academy?"

"I have the afternoon off," said Emily. "All the teachers went to a funeral. I could have gone, but Aunt Cassie has a cold, so I decided to clean house for her." She flicked the broom across the porch. "I'd better get back to work. I have to take the ashes out of the fireplace next."

"Let me help you," said Ben. "That's no work for a girl." In a minute he was up the steps and following her into the house.

Ben knelt at the hearth and began sweeping the ashes together. The gray dust swirled about his head, and he sneezed. The brush struck against a solid object. He pushed at it, but it was caught beneath the andiron. He tugged at it with his fingers, worked it loose, and drew it out.

Resentfully he recognized his inkwell, warped out of shape and covered with gray ash. He was about to drop it in the dustpan when a glint of color caught his eye. He stared at it in disbelief. Where his fingers had come in contact with the glass, small ovals showed a brilliant ruby-red!

In mounting excitement he rubbed the inkwell against his sleeve, and as the ash flaked off, the rich color of the glass shone clear and unmistakable. It was the sought-after golden ruby!

Ben held it out. "Emily, look!" was all he could say.

She took the inkwell from him, her hand trembling. "What a glorious color!" she cried. "I've never seen anything so beautiful!"

"The formula was right, after all," said Ben. He thought of Karl Gantz, thankful that the German had not known his doubt. Now he could guess what the smudged last line of script had said. He repeated softly, "A special property of golden-ruby glass is that—" He paused, then finished triumphantly, "—it must be returned to the fire and reheated."

With a pang, he remembered Martin's suggestion. If the inkwells had been placed in the lehr when they came out of the press, Ben would have known then that the experiment had been a success. Instead, his impatience had caused him days of despair.

Emily's face darkened suddenly, and she burst into tears. "Oh, Ben," she cried, "it's too late. You can never make the golden-ruby glass again! You burned the formula!"

Ben's spirits plummeted. He had been so enthralled by the beauty of the glass that he had forgotten his later action. There, in that very fireplace, he had thrown the formula, the only key to duplicating the glowing ruby color.

How could he have been such a fool? Only an idiot would have acted as he had. Stark dismay smote him, and he let his face fall forward into his hands.

A minute later Emily was shaking his shoulder. He looked up to see her face alight with excitement.

"Ben, do you remember the phoenix?"

"The bird that rose from the ashes after it was burned? What has that got do with ruby glass?"

"Everything, Ben." She held the inkwell toward him. "This is a glass phoenix. It came out of the ashes with new life, more beautiful than ever. It's a sign, Ben. Don't you understand?"

"I don't understand anything except what a fool I was to burn the formula," he said.

"The formula can come out of the ashes with new life, too. You can make it. All you have to do is remember." Her eyes were dancing.

"Remember all those figures? Hardly," said Ben.

"It wouldn't be any more difficult than remembering irregular verbs. How much silex did you use?"

"Twelve pounds," said Ben promptly. He could recall measuring it out.

"And red lead?"

"Nine and three-quarter pounds."

"You see, it's all in your head," said Emily, "just as if it were written down."

She sat at the table and motioned Ben to sit beside her as when they were studying German. Picking up a pen, she started to list the ingredients.

As Ben watched her he began to see the sheet of German script in his mind. If he couldn't remember every ingredient now, perhaps he could later. He was sure he'd be able to recall enough so that he could make a trial batch, and if that was not correct, he could try again and again until he recaptured the exact combination.

Hope and happiness began to well up in him as he looked at Emily. What a wonderful girl she was! Without her he would never have learned that the formula was a success, never have had the courage to try to remember the amounts so that he could make the glass again. Mr. Griswold had certainly been right when he said that every person needed help at some time in his life. Had he known then that his own daughter would be the person who would help Ben the most?

Emily tilted her head toward Ben. "The next time you make golden-ruby glass, would you press an inkwell for me? I could have it on my desk when I'm a teacher."

She had said "the next time" with such confidence that Ben couldn't help but grin.

"I'll make you a dozen, all with a phoenix on each side. The only thing is, I hope you don't intend to be a teacher all your life."

He meant a lot more than that, but with Emily he didn't think he had to spell out each detail.

For a moment she seemed not to comprehend; then her eyes took on a special look that made his heart beat faster, and she said, "Not quite all, Ben."

Her smile told him that she understood.

Ben would have liked nothing better than to stay with Emily. There was a great deal he wanted to talk over with her. But there was someone else to whom he must show the golden-ruby glass, and he shrank from the prospect. Just thinking about it made him feel as queasy as he'd ever felt on board ship. He knew that Karl Gantz had originally intended to sell the ruby-glass formula to Deming Jarves. Although Karl had given it to Ben, he had probably meant that it should be used by the Boston and Sandwich Glass Company. The formula had been almost a sacred trust. How could Ben have been so conceited as to think that he could work it out by himself?

But the longer he put off seeing Mr. Jarves, the harder the meeting would be, so he picked up the inkwell and said, "I'll have to show this to Mr. Jarves."

As always, Emily understood at once. Her eyes full of sympathy, she asked, "How are you going to explain?"

How could *anyone* explain the idiocy of burning the formula?

"I'll just tell him the truth," Ben said, wondering if he sounded as uneasy as he felt.

The way from the Griswold's house to the glassworks had never seemed so short. Ben looked down Dock Lane to the main door of the factory. Mr. Jarves's carriage was not there. Good. Perhaps he had gone to Boston. But a minute later horses' hoofs beat a brisk clip-clop on the road, and the green and yellow vehicle rolled by with a swish of its narrow wheels, its owner austere and lordly on the high seat.

Ben plodded onward, feeling as though each footstep took him nearer to judgment. What would Mr. Jarves say? Worse yet, what would he do? Take away Ben's job, probably. Give orders that he must never enter the factory again? Ben wouldn't blame him for that. He felt as guilty as if he had stolen the formula and destroyed it deliberately.

At the office the sour-faced man kept Ben waiting until he finished totting up a column. Then he said grimly, "What do you want today?"

"To see Mr. Jarves."

"He's busy."

"I'll wait until he can see me," Ben said, and settled himself on a bench.

The man returned to his figures. Ben sat silently, his mind churning. For one wild moment he wished he could dash out the door and away from the office, away from the factory, away from Sandwich. He had half risen to his feet when an inner voice restrained him. He clenched his fists and resumed his wait.

The office door opened, and Mr. Jarves poked his head out. He started to speak to the clerk, then saw Ben. "Good afternoon, Tate. Do you want to see me?"

"Yes, sir." Ben said with a gulp. He followed the older man into the office.

"I hear you'll be working on the pressing machine," Mr. Jarves said. "I expect you and Benson will be making some improvements on it. Won't you sit down?" He waved Ben to a chair.

"No, thank you, sir." For what he must say, Ben needed to stand. He swallowed and tried to speak. No words came. He tried again, and faltered, "I wanted to see you about the golden-ruby glass."

"You remembered what I told you about it?" Mr. Jarves asked. Beneath his courtesy, Ben could sense impatience.

"Not just that," said Ben. Again words failed him. He drew the inkwell out of his pocket and held it toward Mr. Jarves. In the bright sunny office the glass glowed rubylike, its crimson rich and deep. Ben flinched at the amazement and delight on the glass magnate's face.

"By Jove! It's the golden ruby! Where did you get this?" Mr. Jarves cried.

Somehow Ben found his voice, and began his tale

with Karl Gantz's arrival in Sandwich. As the story unfolded, Mr. Jarves grew more and more excited.

Then came the awful moment when Ben must tell
about throwing the formula into the fire. The words
tumbled out, awkward, blunt, and ruthless.

"You *burned the formula?*" Mr. Jarves was incredu-
lous. His face went white, and his lips pulled tight across
his teeth. "Don't you know you should never discard a
formula? You try to find out what part of the process
was wrong, and then you try again."

Ben wilted beneath the man's contemptuous gaze, but
he gathered up the fragments of his courage and said,
"That's what I'd like to do, sir—try again. I've remembered most of the ingredients." He pulled the list from
his pocket, and found strength in Emily's neat handwriting. "Here's the main part of the formula. I'm not
sure about the chemicals to prepare the gold properly,
but I'll try to think of those. And I know now that the
glass must be reheated in the lehr for several hours in
order to bring out the ruby color."

Color came back into Mr. Jarves's face as he studied
the slip of paper. "These amounts look reasonable," he
said. Then he fixed Ben with a penetrating look. "You
know that this formula is practically worthless in its
present state. I cannot offer you anything for it now. But
if it were complete and proven satisfactory, it would be
worth a considerable sum. I might then assign you to
work out more formulas and perhaps have you travel to
other factories in this country and abroad to study
methods. Would that interest you?"

Would it interest him? Ben was almost breathless at

the prospect. Reality sobered him. "I may not be able to remember the chemicals," he blurted. "But if you'd give me a chance to make some trial batches, I might get the right combination again. At least I could try."

Mr. Jarves locked his fingers and studied them. "When you're ready to make another trial, speak to my clerk. I'll give orders that an ounce of gold shall be held in the safe for you. If you need more, come to me about it."

Dazed, Ben could only murmur, "Thank you, sir."

His blue eyes taking on the same sparkle they had held that long-ago day on the *Orion*, Mr. Jarves held out his hand. "I wouldn't be surprised, Tate, if before the year is out the Boston and Sandwich Glass Company might be advertising among its colors the long-sought golden-ruby red."

Just knowing that Mr. Jarves was counting on him gave Ben confidence. Already his mind was reaching to recover the exact number of grams and ounces and pennyweights.

"I'll do my best, sir." Filled with certainty, Ben took Deming Jarves's hand and clasped it firmly, as man to man.

Afterword

Although most of the characters in this story are fictitious, an outstanding exception is Deming Jarves, whose name is synonymous with the great glass factory he founded in Sandwich, Massachusetts, in 1825. Here he manufactured hand-blown glass of the highest quality, much of it exquisitely cut and etched, and pioneered in the production of pressed glass, a low-priced tableware that soon became tremendously popular. Today this tableware, like other types of Sandwich glass, is highly prized by collectors.

Scattered through the book are references to a few other individuals who lived in 1827—Daniel Webster, William Stetson and his family, Captain Fisher, Frederic Tudor, Johnny Trout the Mashpee Indian, and William Fessenden. The packet *Polly* then plied regularly between Sandwich and Boston, and the steamboat *Patent* ran between Eastland and Boston, with stops at ports along the Maine coast.

The dramatic aftermath of the pressing machine's trial stems from a letter written by Deming Jarves:

"The glass blowers, on discovery that I had succeeded in pressing a piece of glass, were so enraged for fear their business would be ruined by the new discovery, that my life was threatened, and I was compelled to hide from them for six weeks before I dared venture in the street or in the glass house, and for more than six months there was danger of personal violence should I venture in the street after nightfall."

Wholly imaginary is Ben Tate's part in the rediscovery of golden-ruby glass in Sandwich. Golden ruby, however, was one of the most prized colors of Sandwich glass. Directions for making it are included in Deming Jarves's book, *Reminiscences of Glass-Making,* which was published in Boston in 1865.

The setting for *The Glass Phoenix* is based on historical facts. Sandwich in 1827 was making a painful transition from farming community to factory town, with friction and hostility separating old-time residents and newcomers. The problems of Sandwich were typical of the young nation's in an era when industry and commerce were developing with all the explosiveness of the fireworks set off by Deming Jarves each year on the Fourth of July. It was an age of grandiose dreams and accomplishments—canals, steamboats, railroads, and other advances.

I like to think that the young men in my story are typical of those encouraged by Deming Jarves in later years to discover different shades of colored glass, and to improve the machines for its pressing. Some were sent to Europe to study manufacturing methods, and some to Boston and other American cities on the recently completed railroads or the *Acorn,* the Boston and Sandwich Glass Company's own steamboat. The quest for what was new and better must have filled their lives with wonder and fascination. Some of that excitement, I hope, is captured in these pages.

About the author

MARY STETSON CLARKE was born and brought up in Melrose, Massachusetts, "in a book-loving family" who encouraged her early efforts to write. After her graduation from Boston University, she spent four exciting years on *The Christian Science Monitor*. She lived in New York City after her marriage, and studied writing at Columbia University while continuing to write feature articles for the *Monitor* and other publications. Except for the few years in the New York area, Mrs. Clarke has lived in Melrose.

While her son and two daughters were in their teens, Mrs. Clarke began writing historical novels; and now that her family is grown, she continues to write for young people. Her earlier books, based on thorough historical research, include *The Iron Peacock, The Limner's Daughter,* and *Petticoat Rebel.*